A NEW COACH

"Kathy really said a new coach might be good for us?" Nikki asked, amazed.

"Yes. Those were her exact words."

"So what do you think that means?" asked Nikki.

"I don't know, except that . . ." Haley hesitated, not wanting even to put it into words. "Do you think Kathy is leaving?"

"Well, she has been acting sort of weird lately. I mean, the way she blew up at you about that joke," Nikki said. "She should be used to your jokes by now."

"And twice I caught her not paying attention during my lesson, like there's something on her mind," Haley added.

"But why would she leave? I thought she loved coaching. Where would she go?" Nikki asked, her voice filled with panic.

"I can't imagine having any coach besides Kathy. If she's leaving, I'll quit. I'll absolutely quit skating," Haley vowed.

RUMORS AT THE RINK

Melissa Lowell

Created by Parachute Press

A SKYLARK BOOK

NEW YORK · TORONTO · LONDON · SYDNEY · AUCKLAND

RL 5, IL ages 9–12

RUMORS AT THE RINK
A Skylark Book / February 1995

Skylark Books is a registered trademark of Bantam Books, a division
of Bantam Doubleday Dell Publishing Group, Inc. Registered in the
U.S. Patent and Trademark Office and elsewhere.

Series design: Barbara Berger

ISBN 0-553-48293-9

Published simultaneously in the United States and Canada

Bantam Books are published by Bantam Books, a division of Bantam Doubleday
Dell Publishing Group, Inc. Its trademark, consisting of the words "Bantam
Books" and the portrayal of a rooster, is Registered in the U.S. Patent and Trademark
Office and in other countries. Marca Registrada. Bantam Books, 1540 Broadway,
New York, New York 10036.

PRINTED IN THE UNITED STATES OF AMERICA

OPM 0 9 8 7 6 5 4 3 2 1

1

Haley Arthur glanced at her skating coach, Kathy Bart, who brought the car to a stop at the red light. Neither of them had said much during the drive home from the Seneca Hills Ice Arena. Haley wondered if Kathy was also thinking about what had happened at the rink that afternoon. Was she replaying the terrible scene again and again in her mind, the way Haley was?

It all started like any ordinary practice session. Well, not exactly, because right before practice Haley decided she hated the way her red bangs always hung in her eyes. She quickly snipped them off—a little too short and a lot too crooked, she realized too late. Her pairs partner and good friend Patrick McGuire joked that Haley was going to start a new fashion craze with her bangs. Haley kidded him back as they worked on a lasso lift. They were perfecting their program for the regional competition five weeks away.

Their skating was going great, and Haley felt their program was really coming together. And then it happened. Haley went into the jump from her left outside edge, but she didn't rotate enough. She landed on her inside edge, and threw them both off balance. Patrick fell. Haley saw his face twist in pain as he grabbed his ankle, and she knew something was terribly wrong.

"I can't stop thinking about it," Haley told Kathy. "What if he broke his ankle? Everything we worked for will be ruined. And even if he just sprained it, how can we practice for the Regionals?"

After only six months of skating together, Patrick and Haley were the best junior pairs couple in the Silver Blades figure-skating club, one of the top clubs in the country. Like most of the other kids in Silver Blades, they dreamed of being Olympic skaters someday. They and the other twenty-five members of the club practiced skating twice a day, every day but Sunday. They started at five-thirty every morning, and returned to the ice after school.

Kathy pulled up in front of Haley's house and turned to face her. "Look. Patrick's at the doctor's right now. I'm sure he'll call you as soon as he knows how his ankle is. Until he does, there's no point in worrying about how bad his injury is or isn't. Whatever happens, we'll deal with it."

"But I feel like it's all my fault," Haley blurted out. "If I hadn't messed up in the takeoff . . ." Her voice trailed off.

"Now, don't start that," Kathy said. "It wasn't your fault. It wasn't Patrick's fault. It wasn't anyone's fault. Accidents happen. It's part of being a serious skater."

Haley frowned. "I know, but it's not fair. We worked so hard. And our program was almost there. Now everything's ruined."

Haley thought about all the practicing they'd done to get each move just right. Would it all be for nothing? Haley knew she and Patrick had a good shot at winning a medal at the upcoming Regionals, their first major competition together. She and her first pairs partner, Michael Bass, had won a gold in the novice Regionals, even though Haley always felt that Michael was not the absolute perfect partner for her.

Then Michael moved to Japan, and Patrick took his place. Almost the second they hit the ice, Haley knew that Patrick was it, her perfect partner. As her friends pointed out, they even looked alike with their red hair and brown eyes.

Kathy put her hand on Haley's shoulder. "Now, listen. Everything is not ruined. You will go on practicing by yourself, and when Patrick's ankle heals, you'll both pick up where you left off. A minor setback, that's all. You better get used to them, because if you're planning to have a professional skating career, you'll have your share of setbacks. Everyone does. The really great skaters are the ones who learn how to handle them."

Haley nodded. She knew Kathy was right, and she also knew that her coach didn't put up with whining for long. Kathy was a tough coach. The kids called her Sarge—never to her face, of course. Sure, Haley groaned about her demanding coach. But she knew Kathy made her try the impossible on the ice—and made sure she succeeded.

"No matter what happens with Patrick, I want to see you back on the ice first thing tomorrow morning, ready to work. Got it?" Kathy said firmly.

"I'll be there," Haley promised.

Kathy smiled. "Okay. "I'll see you tomorrow, then. And try not to worry too much."

Two hours later Haley and her three best friends, Nikki Simon, Tori Carsen, and Danielle Panati, sat in the Arthurs' kitchen, waiting for the phone to ring. Nikki, Tori, and Danielle were also members of Silver Blades, and they had been at the rink that afternoon when Patrick fell. Though it was a Wednesday night and they all had early practice and then school the next day, their parents agreed to let them wait for news from Patrick together at Haley's house.

Haley was glad she had her friends with her. Waiting alone would really drive her crazy.

"When is he going to call?" Tori asked with a groan. She sat slumped over the white kitchen table, resting her chin in one hand, twisting one of her blond curls in the other. Her blue eyes stared at the phone, as if she could will it to ring.

Like Tori, Haley attended Kent Academy, a private school in the town of Burgess, a few minutes away from Seneca Hills. But she was in sixth grade, while Tori, Nikki, and Danielle, who all went to Grandview Middle School, were seventh graders.

"Maybe we should try to call Patrick again," Nikki suggested.

"No," Haley said. "We've already tried twice, and his father sounded kind of mad the last time. He said Patrick will call us as soon as he gets back from the doctor's. We just have to wait."

"But it's already eight o'clock," Danielle said. "I've got to be home soon." She pulled the blue-and-white checkered headband out of her thick honey-brown hair and then replaced it, smoothing her hair into place.

Haley lifted up the receiver and heard her little sister's voice. "Morgan! I told you to stay off the phone," Haley said. "I'm expecting an important call."

"You don't own the phone. This is an important call too," Morgan shot back.

Haley slammed down the receiver and shouted toward the den, "Mom! Please tell Morgan to stay off the phone. We're waiting to hear from Patrick."

"Now, Haley. You're not the only who needs to use the phone. Your sister has to make calls too. Just be patient. You'll find out how he is tomorrow if he doesn't call you tonight."

Haley shook her head and rolled her eyes. "Tomorrow. Can you believe her? As if I'd be able to sleep tonight not knowing."

Nikki's green eyes widened. "Doesn't she get it? Doesn't she understand how important this is?" she whispered.

"My mother thinks that horseback riding is the only sport in the world. She doesn't understand," Haley said. "When she was young she always rode in horse shows, the way Morgan does now. She even rode in a horse show in Madison Square Garden once."

"Well, at least she's not obsessed with your skating the way my mother is with mine," said Tori.

"Yeah, but I wish she acted as if she cared a little more sometimes," Haley said, frowning. "I mean, two years ago, before you moved here, Nikki, my mother suggested I skip afternoon practices because she couldn't pick me up."

The other skaters stared in disbelief.

"This must be one of your jokes," Nikki said. Haley was always playing jokes on them.

"I wish it were," Haley said, "but it happened."

"I can just imagine Kathy's reaction if you told her you couldn't come to afternoon practice anymore," Nikki said.

"I did tell her," Haley continued. "What else could I do? She called my mother and offered to drive me home herself."

"So that's why you ride with Kathy. I always wondered about that," Nikki said.

Haley nodded. She still remembered how angry she was at her mother, and how grateful she was to her coach for her help.

"What's it like riding with the Sarge?" Danielle asked. "Isn't it sort of weird? I mean, what do you talk about?"

Haley shrugged. "The usual. Skating," she said.

"You must talk about something besides skating," Tori said. "Does she ever talk about boyfriends or anything? There's got to be more to her life than just coaching us."

Haley thought for a minute and then shook her head. "She sure isn't going to tell me. I mean, once I asked her if she had a boyfriend. She just looked at me and said, 'What does that have to do with skating?' Anyway, all I need to know is that she placed fourth in the Nationals before she quit competing."

"Why did she quit?" Tori asked.

"I don't know," Haley said.

"Ask her," Tori said.

"Why don't you?" Haley said, getting a little impatient.

"Because she doesn't give me a ride home every day," Tori replied.

"Hey, all I know is she's a great coach and I don't know what I'd do without her, okay?" Haley picked up the receiver again, ready to yell at Morgan, no matter what her mother said. But she heard the dial tone instead. "She's off. Patrick should be calling any minute."

"I can't take much more of this waiting," Nikki said. "Let's do something fun."

"Let's make some popcorn," suggested Danielle. She crossed the kitchen and pulled opened a cabinet. "Don't you have any microwave popcorn?"

"It's over there. In that one," Haley told her, pointing at another cabinet on the other side of the stove.

Suddenly the phone rang. "That's him!" Haley cried, grabbing the receiver.

"Patrick?" she said. "Is it broken?" She crossed her fingers and squeezed her eyes shut, waiting for the news.

"Well, it's not broken, just sprained," her partner replied. He didn't sound so happy about it.

"But, Patrick, that's great!" Haley felt relief wash over her. She cupped her hand over the receiver and told her friends the good news. The others cheered as Haley waved at them to be quiet. "I was scared that you broke it," she added.

"Yeah, well, it's almost as bad," Patrick said. "I have to stay off the ice for a month."

"A month?" Haley asked.

"Yeah. It stinks, doesn't it?" Patrick said.

"A month . . ." Haley repeated. "That gives us only a week to get ready for the Regionals."

"Don't you think I know that?" Patrick snapped. "It's not like I planned it, you know."

Haley was so shocked by Patrick's outburst that she couldn't think of a thing to say. He must be really upset about the accident. And it was all her fault. "Patrick, look, I'm awfully sorry about what happened, but there will be other competitions and we—"

"I don't want to talk about it right now," Patrick said, cutting her off. "I'm really tired. Maybe I'll come by the rink tomorrow."

"Okay," Haley said as she heard the receiver click in her ear.

She slowly hung up the phone and told the others what Patrick said. "I've never heard him sound so down," she finished.

"He's usually always in a good mood," Danielle said.

"Well, you'd feel bad too if the accident had happened to you," Nikki pointed out.

"True, but at least Haley still has a skating partner," Tori said.

Haley nodded. She was glad it was only a sprain. But one week to prepare for the Regionals wasn't enough time. It was so unfair. They had had a shot at winning, and now . . . well, she couldn't think about it.

"Like Kathy said, it's just a minor setback," Haley said, trying to sound cheerful. "But I have a feeling it's going to be a *very long* month."

The next morning, as Haley warmed up for her lesson, she eagerly looked around the rink for Patrick. Why is he late? she wondered. Then she remembered the accident. This feels so weird, she thought. It was going to be hard skating without him. After all, for three years she had always skated with a partner.

Across the rink she saw Nikki and her pairs partner, Alex Beekman, working on their new program. She watched as they executed a flawless star lift and then went into a pair sit spin. Haley waved to Nikki, and the two of them skated over to her. Alex ran a hand through his dark curly hair. "Hey, I heard about Patrick. Is he really off the ice for a month?"

Haley nodded. "But at least his ankle's not broken."

"Yeah, but a month . . . he's going to go nuts!" Alex skated in a backward circle around Nikki and Haley.

"Do you have a lesson now?" Nikki asked.

"Yes," Haley said, "but Kathy's not here yet."

"That's weird. She's never late. And when we're late she acts as if we should be thrown out of Silver Blades," Nikki said with a laugh that showed a mouth full of braces.

Before Haley could answer, she spotted Kathy hurrying toward the ice. Alex and Nikki went back to work and Haley skated over to Kathy.

"Hi. Ready to go to work?" Kathy asked her.

"Yeah, but it sure feels strange. I think I've forgotten how to skate alone."

"You'll get used it," Kathy assured her. "And it's just for a month. It might be good for you to strengthen your single work. Then you can include more side-by-side jumps in your program. I think we'll work on your double axel today. It would be nice to have a double axel in your pairs program."

"But I've never landed a double axel. And if I do, we'll have only a week to practice it together when Patrick gets back on the ice," Haley protested.

She expected her coach to lecture her about her complaining, but Kathy just stared off across the rink, not even listening to what Haley was saying.

"Kathy?" Haley said.

Kathy looked at her. "Oh. Guess you should get started."

Haley shrugged, skated out to the middle of the rink, and circled for a few minutes. When she felt ready she pushed off from her left outside edge, pulled her arms in quickly to her sides, and rose into the air. She spun, once, twice, and then down, landing with a thud on her backside.

"Not enough height," Kathy called. "Try it again. This time get your arms in faster."

Haley tried the jump again and again but always came just short of landing it. By the end of her lesson she felt tired and frustrated. I'm not ready for this jump, Haley thought. Why is Kathy pushing me to do it?

Finally Kathy called, "Okay. That's enough for today. Use the rest of the time to work on your footwork for the pairs program."

Haley practiced the intricate footwork pattern, but without Patrick she felt awkward and off balance. Yesterday, before the accident, she and Patrick had changed some of the footwork, so she wanted Kathy to review the new steps. She skated over to her coach.

"You know the last sequence of our program?" Haley began, but Kathy paid no attention. She was again staring off across the ice.

"Uh, Kathy," Haley said.

Kathy turned to her, then looked at her watch. "Oh. Is it time already? Okay. That's enough for today. We'll keep working on that double axel. You'll land it soon."

For the first time ever, Kathy didn't sound convincing, but almost halfhearted.

Haley nodded and skated over to Nikki and Alex. "Boy, Kathy sure is in a weird mood today. It's like her mind is somewhere else," Haley said. "She hardly paid any attention to me."

"Really? Usually she's so focused during lessons, we can't get away with anything," Nikki replied.

"I know. It's really strange. I hope nothing's wrong with her," Haley said with concern.

"I wonder what she was thinking about," Nikki said.

"Maybe she's just upset about Patrick," Alex reasoned.

"Could be," Haley said as the three of them skated to the side of the rink and left the ice.

That afternoon, just as Haley finished her second practice session, she spotted Patrick. He hobbled on crutches toward the stands. Haley saw that his normally cheerful face was twisted in a frown as he slowly made his way forward.

"Patrick!" Haley shouted as she skated over to the barrier.

Patrick turned around but didn't try to move toward her. "I'm not used to these crutches yet," he explained. "The doctor said it'll get a lot easier." He sat down heavily on the bench and stretched his bad ankle out in front of him, propping his crutches beside him. "I'm not supposed to put any weight on it for at least a week," he added.

"That gives you a chance to build up your arm muscles with those crutches so you can lift me higher," Haley joked, trying to cheer him up.

But Patrick didn't smile. "It's not funny, Haley," he said. "It hurts."

"Does it hurt a lot?" Haley looked closely at the swollen ankle. It was wrapped in a white bandage. Patrick had pulled a red sock over it and wore no shoe on that foot.

"Only when I have to move it, or put weight on it," he said.

"Well, I can sign your bandage," Haley tried another joke.

Patrick just glared at her. Haley's eyes widened and for a second she thought she would cry. Patrick always joked around. That was one of the reasons the two were such good friends. Haley always said playing jokes ran in her family. Her father loved jokes, and he loved to be tricked by her. Then she discovered she could make the kids in school laugh. She found that playing jokes and being funny was a great way to make friends and be popular, and she never hurt anybody. But her jokes with Patrick sure were backfiring.

"Look, I know you're trying to cheer me up," Patrick said, "but I guess this ankle thing's got me down. I mean, one whole month off the ice is a long time!"

"But you'll get right back in shape," Haley said. She plunked down onto the bench beside Patrick and stretched her legs out in front of her. "Last night, before you called I was so . . . worried. I couldn't believe it. It all happened so fast. . . ."

Patrick nodded. "I know. We had that jump nailed. We've done it a hundred times."

"It was my fault," Haley said. "I messed up on the takeoff and threw us off balance."

"Nah. It's no one's fault. I just wish we could do an instant replay and take it all back," Patrick said sadly.

They watched Nikki and Alex practicing the star lift. "They've got good height, but our star lift is smoother than theirs," Patrick commented.

Haley nodded. Too bad we won't be working on it for a month, she thought, but she said, "Of course we're smoother. We're the best." And she held out her hand so he could slap her five, then she slapped him back and they did a high five. This always worked to cheer them up.

"So, how was practice?" he asked.

Haley shrugged. "I'm working on the double axel. Kathy says I'll land it soon."

"So you don't mind skating alone?" he asked.

"To tell you the truth, it's awful without you. But it's also true that I need to work on my single skating," she said. "Anyway, it's only for four weeks. I can take it if you can."

"I don't know if I can," Patrick muttered, eyeing his bandaged ankle.

Just then Nikki and Tori spotted them and came over. Nikki sat down next to Patrick. "Hey, I don't blame you for wanting to get away from Haley for a while, but isn't there a better way?" she said. "I mean, trying to break your ankle is a bit extreme, don't you think?"

"Yeah. But look at the bright side," Tori added. "You won't have to listen to Sarge yelling at you for a whole month." She quickly looked around to see if the coach was within hearing distance.

"And you won't have to wake up at five o'clock in the morning," Nikki continued. "It'll be like a vacation."

"Maybe I'll sprain my ankle too," Haley said with a laugh.

When Patrick didn't respond to their teasing, Haley gave her friends a warning look to stop. For a while no one spoke, then Patrick looked at his watch. "I've got to get to work," he said.

"You're working today?" Tori asked.

Patrick nodded.

Tori and Haley looked at each other. Patrick worked part-time in the ice arena snack bar. Haley didn't see how he would manage the job on crutches. She wondered what Harry Nelson, Patrick's boss at the snack bar, would say. "Does Harry know about your ankle?" she asked.

"I don't know. He's probably heard by now," Patrick said.

"Do you think you can work on crutches?" Nikki asked.

"I don't have a choice. I can't lose this job. I need the money to help pay for my skating lessons, and there are a lot of other kids who are dying to get my job. If I let one of them take over now, I may never get it back." Patrick hoisted himself up slowly. "I'll make it somehow."

"We'll come over as soon as we get changed," Haley said. They watched him hobble off.

"He can hardly walk on those things. How can he work? You know how crazy it can get in there," Tori said, shaking her head.

"Do you think Harry will fire him?" Nikki asked.

"I hope not," Haley said. "If he loses his job, it would be the worst. He'd have to quit skating."

As soon as they changed out of their practice clothes, Haley, Nikki, and Tori headed for the snack bar.

"Looks like the Hawks have descended," Haley commented as they searched for seats. The Seneca Hills Hawks was the hockey team that practiced on the arena's second rink. Practice just ended, and several players sat at the snack bar.

"Hey, Patrick, I ordered a Coke twenty minutes ago!" shouted one of the players.

"It's coming, it's coming," Patrick told him. Haley watched as Patrick leaned his crutches against the counter, picked up a plate with a burger on it, and hopped on his good foot over to Todd Simpson.

"Can I get cheese on this?" Todd asked as Patrick set the plate down.

"Sure," Patrick muttered. He took the burger back, slapped a piece of cheese on it, and put it under the broiler. As it cooked, he grabbed his crutches and hobbled over to the soda machine. Resting his shoulders on his crutches, he filled a glass with Coke. Haley, seated at the counter with Tori and Nikki, saw that Patrick's face was beaded with sweat. She watched him take an order from some kids who just came in. By the time he hopped back to the broiler, smoke poured from it and the cheeseburger was black.

"Just forget it. I'm not hungry anymore," Todd said when he saw the burned burger.

Alex Beekman leaned across the counter and grabbed his Coke from the fountain. "Hey, Alex, you can't do that," Patrick said.

"I'm just trying to help. If I wait for you to bring it to me, I'll die of thirst."

As Haley watched how bad things were going for Patrick, she got a sinking feeling. "We'd better not order anything," she whispered to her friends, "it's too hard for Patrick to move."

"I don't think this is going to work," Nikki whispered back.

"Maybe it'll get better when he gets used to the crutches," Haley said hopefully, but she doubted it. It just wasn't possible to move quickly on crutches.

Behind the counter Patrick piled the order for the other table on a tray. Using one hand, he tried to carry it across the room with only one crutch. Haley was about to help him, when he slipped and dropped the whole tray.

Alex started to laugh. Immediately Patrick turned on him. "You think this is fun?" he yelled. "Why don't you try it!" He grabbed his crutch and threw it down at Alex's feet.

"Uh-oh," said Haley. She ran to the tray of spilled food and started cleaning up the mess. Patrick hopped back behind the counter and Tori hurried to pick up his crutch.

Patrick's boss, Harry, heard the noise and came out of the little office to the side of the snack bar. "What's going on out here? If you guys get rowdy, you'll have to leave." Harry was short and bald, with a big belly. Though he sometimes sounded gruff, the kids knew he loved them.

"Patrick slipped, that's all," Haley told him.

Harry patted Patrick's shoulder. "I said you wouldn't be able to work on crutches. Look, I'll take over. You go home and take it easy."

"It's just a sprained ankle. I can handle it," Patrick protested.

"Yeah, yeah. Well, today I'll handle it. But tomorrow Timmy will take over for you. He already offered to take over your hours."

Timmy also worked at the snack bar. Haley knew Timmy wanted to work more hours—wanted to take over Patrick's shift.

"But, Harry, I need this job," Patrick cried.

"I'm sorry, but it just isn't going to work. No one can do this job on crutches. Now, go on and get out of here," Harry instructed.

Haley saw the look of frustration on Patrick's face as he turned away, and she knew she had to do something. If Patrick lost his job, she'd lose Patrick as a skating partner.

"Wait—Harry," Haley spoke up suddenly. "Listen, maybe I could fill in, just until Patrick gets better.

That way he can keep his job, and Timmy won't be overloaded."

"Really?" Patrick asked. "Can you really do it?"

"Sure. I mean, I've never worked in a snack bar before, but I think I can handle it. I have to ask my mom, but I'm sure she'll say yes."

Harry stared at Haley, his head tilted to one side, then he looked at Patrick. Finally he nodded. "Okay. We'll give it a try. Be here Monday at five, right after practice. Timmy and I will train you for the first few days. And be prepared for a crowd. Everyone leaves the rink and heads directly to the snack bar. They're hungry and thirsty, and you'll be the one who has to take care of them all."

"No problem," Haley assured him. "I'll be here." She looked forward to it. After all, how hard could working at the snack bar be?

3

The next day, Friday, Haley arrived a few minutes late for morning practice. Almost everyone else was out on the ice, so they didn't notice her. Good, she thought. Preparing herself had taken a lot longer than usual. But she couldn't wait to see the other kids' reactions when they saw her. She laughed to herself as she hurried toward the rink.

Tori was the first to notice. "Haley! What happened?" she cried, skating over to Haley by the edge of the rink. Nikki and Danielle followed her. They stared in shock at the white plaster cast on Haley's arm.

"A cast? Is it broken?" asked Nikki in a panicked voice.

Haley tried to look as if she were in pain, and nodded. "It happened last night. I was wrestling with

Morgan and I fell off the top bunk in her room. Mom had to rush me to the emergency room." It took all of Haley's control to keep from laughing as her friends stared in horror at the cast on her arm.

"What's going on here?" Kathy asked.

"Uh-oh. Wait till she sees this," Tori whispered.

Kathy's smile faded when she saw the cast. She stared at Haley. "Oh, no! Don't tell me. Not you too," she cried.

Haley nodded. She repeated the same story she had told her friends.

"I don't believe it. First Patrick and now you. We must be jinxed." Kathy put her arm around Haley. "What hospital did you go to?"

Haley thought quickly. "Umm, Grandview Memorial," she told them.

"And what did the doctor say? Is it a bad fracture?" Kathy asked.

"Yes. It's bad. Very bad," Haley replied. "I have to wear the cast for at least six weeks."

"Six weeks! Well, there go the Regionals." Kathy frowned and shook her head. "But why are you dressed for skating?" she asked Haley. "You know you can't skate with a broken arm."

Haley couldn't control herself any longer. She burst out laughing, and the puzzled looks on her friends' faces made her laugh even harder.

"All right, Haley. What's going on here?" Kathy demanded.

Haley whipped the cast off her arm. "Gotcha."

Nikki, Tori, and Danielle started giggling, but Kathy was not amused. "Haley," she snapped, "I thought I made it clear to you that we don't have time for juvenile pranks."

Nikki, Danielle, and Tori stopped laughing and glanced at one another. Kathy was mad. Real mad.

"Listen to me," Kathy went on in a stern voice. "You've wasted our valuable lesson time with your joke. There are plenty of other skaters who would like to be in this club. If you can't take it seriously, maybe you shouldn't be skating. Now let's get to work. And the next time you get the urge to play a practical joke, I advise you to think twice." Kathy turned abruptly and marched out onto the ice.

"Wow! She went ballistic," Nikki whispered to Haley as they skated into the middle of the rink.

"It was just a joke. I just wanted to pep things up a bit," Haley said. "Practice is so boring without Patrick, and he's been out only two days."

Tori and Danielle caught up to them and Danielle said, "Well, I thought it was funny. Where'd you get the cast? It looks so real."

"I got it at the House of Magic," Haley told her. "It's the coolest shop. They've got everything. Practical jokes, magic tricks, costumes."

"Haley's heaven," said Danielle.

"It is. I love that place."

"Uh-oh. She's probably got a whole new supply of jokes. We'd better watch it," Nikki teased.

"Well, one thing's for sure," Haley said. "I won't be playing any more jokes when Kathy's around."

During practice Haley worked hard on her double axel, trying again and again. Though she still couldn't land the jump, she felt that she was getting closer. She hoped that Kathy saw how hard she was working, but when she looked across the rink to Kathy's usual spot, her coach wasn't there. Where was she?

Finally Haley spotted her sitting in the stands with a woman Haley didn't know. Is she a scout? Haley wondered. But it didn't make sense for a scout to come here. They usually looked for talented skaters at competitions.

The woman followed Kathy down out of the stands. They stopped at the barrier, talking. Haley just had to know what they were saying. She skated over to side, crouched by the barrier, and pretended to retie her boot lace. "They look like nice kids," she heard the woman say to Kathy. "I'm sure I'll enjoy working with them."

"I think it will be great. I've been here so long, and they're all so used to me. A new coach might be good for them. I just hope everything works out with Amy," Kathy said.

A new coach? What is she talking about? Haley wondered. And who is Amy?

Haley wondered what Kathy meant all day long. For once she wished she weren't so curious.

When she returned to the rink after school, she went straight to Kathy's office. She wanted to apologize for the trick she had pulled that morning. Kathy's door was ajar. Haley knocked lightly. Kathy spun around and saw her. "Haley. Come in," she said. "What can I do for you?"

"Umm, I, ah, I just wanted to apologize. I—I'm really sorry about the cast and all. Sometimes I can't help playing jokes. But I really am serious about skating. . . ."

"Oh, I know you are. I've got a lot on my mind lately, and I don't need practical jokes right now. But I accept your apology and that's all we'll say about it. Okay?"

"Okay," Haley said softly.

Kathy held out the newspaper in her hand and pointed to an article. "Look, it's about the Ice Follies."

Haley read the headline. "PRO SKATERS PERFORM IN ICE FOLLIES SHOW."

"They're coming to town next week, you know," Kathy said.

"I know. Are you going?" Haley asked.

"I wouldn't miss it. And guess what? My friend Amy Benson is the featured skater this year. I can't wait to see her perform," Kathy said, her eyes sparkling.

"Wow. That's so exciting. How do you know her?"

"We've been friends for ages. We skated together for years," Kathy explained as she folded the newspaper and put it carefully in her desk drawer.

Amy, thought Haley. I wonder if that's the Amy she mentioned to that woman earlier. What did Kathy mean, "if everything works out with Amy"?

Haley wanted to ask Kathy, but she didn't dare. All she needed now was to get Kathy mad at her all over again by asking her about something she wasn't even supposed to have heard.

"Well, it's time to hit the ice and get to work," Kathy announced.

In her room later that night, Haley tried to do her homework, but Kathy's words about a new coach being good for the skaters kept running through her mind.

She closed her history book and leaned back in her chair. Earlier she'd made a halfhearted attempt to clean up her room, but she had to admit, it didn't look much better. She stared at her unmade bed, the black and white striped bedspread spilling off onto the floor. Her clothes and books were scattered haphazardly around the room. A bunch of her old stuffed animals were stacked on the extra chair. She meant to pack them away or give them to Morgan, but somehow she kept putting it off.

She eyed her wall that was covered with a collage of skater pictures and posters. Her mother had had a fit when she first saw it, but it was worth it. It looked so cool.

Her favorite photographs sat on the dresser. There were some of her family, and one of herself, Tori, Nikki, Danielle, and their friend Jill Wong, taken last summer at skating camp. Her eyes rested on the picture of Kathy giving Haley a big hug just after she won a medal at the last competition. As she stared at the photo, she relived the thrill of winning the medal. It was thanks to Kathy's coaching that I won, she thought. And instantly the conversation she'd overheard earlier popped back into her mind. Haley's smile faded.

I've got to talk to someone, she decided. She called Nikki and told her everything she'd overheard between Kathy and the woman.

"Kathy really said a new coach might be good for us?" Nikki asked, amazed.

"Yes. Those were her exact words."

"What did the woman look like?"

"She's about Kathy's age, and she was wearing a warm-up suit." Haley took the phone over to her bed and flopped down on her back.

"So what do you think it means?" asked Nikki.

"I don't know, except that . . ." Haley hesitated, not wanting even to put it into words. "Do you think Kathy is *leaving*?"

"Well, she has been acting sort of weird lately. I mean, the way she blew up at you about that joke," Nikki said. "She should be used to your jokes by now."

"And twice I caught her not paying attention during my lesson, like there's something on her mind," Haley added.

"But why would she leave? I thought she loved

coaching. Where would she go?" Nikki asked, her voice filled with panic.

"I can't imagine having any coach besides Kathy. If she's leaving, I'll quit. I'll absolutely quit skating," Haley vowed.

"She can't be leaving. I don't believe it. You must have misunderstood her," Nikki insisted.

"Yeah, maybe . . ." Haley hoped Nikki was right. "Listen, there's something else I need to talk to you about. You know how Patrick's been so down since the accident?"

"I'll say. He's like a walking rain cloud. He makes you sad just looking at him," Nikki said.

"Let's do something to cheer him up."

"Like what?" Nikki asked.

"Maybe we could throw a party for him," Haley suggested.

"Great idea! What about a surprise party?"

"Sounds good to me. Let's talk to Danielle and Tori about it tomorrow. I'm sure they'll want to help," Haley said, sitting up.

"Okay. Right now I've got to go. Mom's yelling for me. She's on the warpath lately," Nikki said a little resentfully. Nikki was an only child, used to being the center of attention, but ever since her mom got pregnant, Nikki said her mom's moods swung between always hugging her and constantly yelling at her. Haley understood what it was like. Up until Morgan came along, Haley was the center of attention in the family. But now it sometimes seemed that Morgan's horseback riding was all her mom ever talked about.

The two friends hung up, and Haley felt a little better. Maybe she had misunderstood Kathy, like Nikki said. Whatever it was, tomorrow she planned to keep her eyes and ears open—and find out for sure what was really going on.

Haley, Tori, Nikki, and Danielle sat in the snack bar after their Saturday lesson.

"I think a party is a great idea. It should cheer Patrick up," Tori agreed.

"We'll all chip in and buy the pizza," Haley said.

"I can ask my grandmother to bake some stuff too," Danielle said. Danielle's grandmother lived with the Panati family and was famous with Danielle's friends for her great desserts.

"Awesome. Nikki and I think it should be a surprise, don't you?" Haley asked.

"Definitely," Tori said. "I love surprise parties! Let's talk to Kathy about when we can do it. She'll help us get permission to use the snack bar."

"Speaking of Kathy," said Nikki, glancing at Haley as she sipped her iced tea, "Have you told them?"

"Told us what?" asked Tori, looking from Haley to Nikki. Tori couldn't stand it when the others knew something she didn't.

Haley repeated the conversation she'd overheard between Kathy and the other woman.

"Wow!" said Danielle. "Does this mean what I think it means?"

"Is Kathy leaving?" Tori asked.

"Let's hope not," said Nikki.

"Maybe you heard wrong," Tori said. "Are you sure you heard her say a new coach would be good for us?"

"I think so . . . but maybe not." Haley really wanted to believe that she was mistaken, though she was pretty sure she wasn't.

Danielle frowned. "Can't you just ask her? I mean, she drives you home every day."

"Sure," Haley said. "I'll just come out and ask her and she'll just bite my head off."

"I guess it wouldn't be such a good idea," Danielle admitted. "But maybe we can get some more clues and figure out what's going on."

"Good idea," said Tori. "I love playing detective. This could be fun."

Fun? How could Tori say this was fun? Haley thought. Didn't she realize how serious the whole thing was. If Kathy left, well, it was too awful to think about. Of course, it wouldn't be so bad for Tori and Danielle. Franz Weiler coached them, not Kathy.

"There's Alex," Nikki said, waving to him as he walked into the snack bar. "Let's tell him about the party."

Alex squeezed into the booth next to Nikki. "I saw you guys whispering over here. What's going on?"

"We're planning a party for Patrick. Something to cheer him up," Haley explained.

"Cool. He could use some cheering up," said Alex. "When is it going to be?"

"We don't know yet. We have to talk to Kathy. The only thing we know for sure is we want it to be here in the snack bar, and it's going to be a surprise party."

"Uh-oh. I think he heard us," Danielle whispered, staring at something above Haley's head.

"Who?" said Haley, turning around. Patrick was standing right behind her!

"So what's up?" he asked. He propped his crutches against the wall and eased himself into the booth next to Danielle.

"Nothing. Nothing new. Just the same stuff," said Nikki, her face turning pink.

"Right. We were just talking about . . . umm, the party that my sister is having. For her birthday," Haley said quickly.

"Morgan? It's her birthday?" Patrick asked.

"Right. It's a surprise party. She's really excited about it," Haley continued.

"Well, if it's a surprise party, how can she be excited about it?" Patrick asked.

"Well, she's excited about her birthday coming up.

You know how kids her age are about their birthdays." Whoa, I'm really blowing it, Haley thought.

"How old is she?" asked Patrick.

"Ten and a half," Haley said without thinking. "I mean . . . she *was* ten and a half. Now she's almost eleven. She'll be eleven on her birthday, of course . . . but I got confused, you know . . . I forget that she's almost eleven. They do grow fast, don't they . . ." Haley realized that she was making things worse, but she couldn't seem to stop talking.

Patrick shot Haley a puzzled look, reached for his crutches, and stood up. "Well, I gotta go. I'm going to work with Ernie in the weight room. Trying to keep my strength up. See you."

As he slowly hobbled off, Alex shook his head and laughed. "Come on, Haley. That was really lame."

"I know. I couldn't stop myself. I wasn't making any sense at all," Haley moaned.

"It's not going to be easy keeping this party a secret," Nikki said.

"Yeah, we just came up with the idea, and we almost blew it already," Danielle said.

When they finished their drinks, Haley, Nikki, Danielle, and Tori left the snack bar and went to Kathy's office to talk to her about the party.

"Maybe we can do a little spying while we're there," Tori said. "Keep your eyes open for anything suspicious."

They found Kathy at her desk, and Haley saw she

was reading the same newspaper article about the Ice Follies.

"Well, if it isn't the four musketeers. What can I do for you guys?"

They told Kathy all about their plan for the party.

"I think it's a great idea," Kathy said. "Patrick certainly is down in the dumps, and a party might be just the thing to cheer him up."

"We'll pay for everything, but do you think we could have it here at the rink?" Haley asked.

"I don't see why not. I'll check with Harry and Mr. Weiler, but I'm sure they'll agree," Kathy said. "When do you want to have it?"

"Well, we should probably wait until Patrick can manage better on crutches," Haley said.

"What about two Saturdays from today?" Danielle asked.

Kathy checked her calendar. "I've got something scheduled that night," she said. "How about the following Saturday?"

"Sounds good," Haley agreed.

Tori looked over Kathy's shoulder at her newspaper. "Oh. You're reading about the Ice Follies. I can't wait to see them," she said with excitement.

"Yes. And this article highlights my friend Amy Benson. She's the headliner this year," Kathy said.

"She must be a fantastic skater," said Tori.

"She is," Kathy said. "We skated together for years."

"Was she in the Nationals like you?" Danielle asked.

"Yes. She came in sixth the year I was fourth,"

Kathy told them. "Listen to this," she said, reading from the article. " 'Ms. Benson spent the summer and early fall touring Europe with the Follies. The show was a hit, selling out in almost every city they visited. They are hoping that the U.S. tour will be as successful, and judging by the first two weeks, it will be.' "

"Wow!" said Tori.

"Sounds pretty glamorous, doesn't it?" Kathy commented.

"Did you ever think about joining the Follies?" asked Nikki. All four girls waited expectantly for the coach's answer.

Kathy studied the paper for a minute. "I almost joined back when Amy did," she said. "But I wanted some coaching experience, and when this job came up, I took that instead." She shook her head, staring at the picture of Amy. "And now look at Amy. The top skater in the Follies."

"Would you ever, you know, reconsider?" Haley asked. She was almost afraid to ask the question for fear of Kathy's answer.

But Kathy just laughed. "What, and give all this up? How can Paris, London, and New York compare to Seneca Hills?"

"Besides, you could never leave your devoted students, right, Kathy?" Danielle asked half-jokingly.

"Ha." Kathy smiled. "Sometimes I think you guys would all be better off without me." She put her arm around Danielle and gave her a playful squeeze. "Now, out of here. All of you. I've got work to do, and so do you!"

As soon as they were out of earshot, Haley whispered, "Is she kidding? Or do you think she means it? Do you think she really likes it here?"

"I think she really does," said Danielle.

"I don't know," Tori said. "Why would she want to stay here when she could be touring Europe? It looks to me like Nikki and Haley might be getting a new coach."

Tori sounds almost happy about it, Haley thought. Like she doesn't even care.

"You don't know anything about it, Tori. You hardly even know Kathy," Haley said.

"Well, maybe I don't know her as well as you do, but I'm not dumb," Tori said. "I mean, look at the facts. You're the one who heard her say a new coach would be good for us. And we all heard how excited she is about Amy Benson and the Ice Follies."

"So? Just because she's talking about the Ice Follies doesn't mean she wants to join them," Haley said. She wished Tori would just be quiet.

But Tori went on. "And anyway, she's really grouchy lately. Look at the way she yelled at you when you pulled that joke with the cast. I never saw her so mad."

Tori stopped just outside the door to the locker room and turned to Haley. "Let's face it," Tori said with a shrug. "If you had a choice between coaching us and being in the Ice Follies, which one would *you* choose?"

Monday morning Haley grabbed the small laugh box her dad had given her as a present from his last business trip and shoved it in her jacket pocket. For once she had a real excuse for bringing one of her tricks with her to the rink. She was using it for a skit in English class that afternoon.

After the morning practice the members of Silver Blades sat in the bleachers listening closely to every word the two coaches, Kathy Bart and Franz Weiler, and the new choreographer, Blake Michaels, said about the upcoming Regional skating competition in four weeks.

"This is an important competition for many reasons," Kathy said. As the coach explained about Regionals, and which levels everyone was skating in, Haley watched the other members of the club. Just like her, she knew they all hoped that this competition would make them a star.

Haley imagined herself and Patrick, just the two of them on the ice, everyone focused on them. In her daydream they moved through their program perfectly, their timing just right. When they completed a flawless death spiral, they both knew they won, and when they finished, the thundering applause proved it.

Haley turned to Patrick, but he was staring at his sprained ankle.

"Haley and Patrick! Listen up!" Kathy demanded.

Haley nodded, thinking that they would be lucky to skate at all, and that their chances of winning were slim to none. How could they win with only one week to get ready?

"Haley and Patrick," Kathy repeated. "We're going to wait and see what happens with Patrick's ankle. If it heals well, and it looks like you're both ready, you'll skate. If not, well, there are plenty of other competitions. For now, Haley, you'll keep working on your jumps and the footwork sequence, and Patrick, you keep your strength up in the weight room, and we'll see what happens."

Haley glanced over at Patrick, but he didn't look her way. If the ankle heals well, Kathy said. But what if it didn't? What if Patrick never got his full strength back in his ankle? Haley had heard plenty of stories about injuries just like this one that ruined careers. But it will heal well, she told herself. It has to!

When Kathy announced that Danielle was skating in the Junior Ladies singles, Haley reached over to give her friend's hand a squeeze, and accidentally hit the laugh box in her jacket pocket. A loud screeching laugh roared through the bleachers.

Haley felt the color rise to her cheeks. Quickly she turned the laugh box off, but by then it was too late. Everyone had burst out laughing. Everyone but Kathy. Kathy definitely wasn't laughing. In fact, Kathy looked furious.

She glared at Haley. "We don't have time for interruptions," she said. "I thought I had made that clear, Haley. Please leave the meeting. I'll talk to you about this when we're done."

"B-but it was an accident . . ." Haley stuttered.

"Not now. Please do as I say," Kathy commanded.

Haley stood up and squeezed her way past the other kids. She felt her face burning, and she was afraid she was going to start crying right in front of everyone. She ran to the locker room and sat down on the bench. Why was Kathy so angry? She hadn't meant to do it. She totally forgot that the laugh box was in her pocket. It wasn't her fault it had gone off in the middle of the meeting.

A few minutes later Nikki, Danielle, and Tori burst into the locker room.

"Is it over?" Haley asked.

"Yeah, and Kathy's looking for you. Boy, is she angry," Tori said.

"I didn't mean to do it, really. The thing was in my

pocket and it just went off," Haley explained to her friends.

Nikki started to laugh. "I'll never forget the look on Kathy's face when that screeching started. It was so funny."

"I'd better go find her and try to apologize," Haley said.

"Good luck," Danielle said. "You're going to need it."

Haley caught up with Kathy outside her office. "There you are," Kathy said. "Now, listen here, Haley. I've had just about enough of your pranks. This is getting out of hand. There's nothing wrong with having a sense of humor, but when it begins to interfere with the serious business of skating, it's time to stop."

"But I didn't mean to do it, really . . . it was in my pocket and—"

"I don't want to hear excuses, I just want it stopped," Kathy cut her off. "Have I made myself clear?"

Haley nodded. "I'm really sorry. It won't happen again," she promised.

"See that it doesn't," Kathy said, entering her office and closing the door.

Haley walked back to the locker room.

"How'd it go?" asked Danielle.

"She's really mad. I never saw her like this. You'd think I said I hated skating, the way she's acting. I mean, it was just a joke. And I didn't even mean to do it this time," Haley insisted.

"I know," Nikki agreed. "She's not acting like herself. Something's definitely wrong."

"And we've got to find out what," said Haley.

That afternoon after practice Haley worked with Timmy for an hour at the snack bar. He grilled the burgers, and showed her how to work the soda machine and make sandwiches. There weren't a lot of people at the snack bar, and Haley felt that the job was pretty easy. That night when her mom picked her up, she tried to tell her about it. But Morgan was in the car, and all they talked about was horses. As they pulled into Haley's driveway, Haley wished for about the millionth time that her mom would for once care as much about her skating.

Thursday morning after practice the girls passed Kathy's office on their way to the locker room when Tori stopped just outside the coach's door. She put her finger to lips and signaled for quiet. "I heard her say 'Amy.' Maybe she's talking to her on the phone."

"It must be important if she's calling so early," Haley whispered back.

"We shouldn't eavesdrop," Danielle said in a low voice.

"But we have to find out what's going on with her. What if she really is leaving?" Tori pointed out.

The girls huddled outside the office. "Oh, that sounds great, Amy," they heard Kathy say. "I can't wait to tour with you. Only four weeks to go." There was a pause, and then Kathy said, "Hang on a minute. I think someone's at my door."

"She's coming," Haley whispered. In a panic she whipped open the door of the supply closet next to Kathy's office. It was a big walk-in closet with plenty of space for the four of them. "Quick. In here," Haley urged, motioning the others to hurry.

They scrambled inside and closed the door just as they heard Kathy coming out. "Hello? Anyone out here?" Kathy called.

After a minute the girls heard her close her office door, and through the wall came the muffled sound of her voice.

"Whew! Was that ever close," whispered Danielle. "Do you know what she'd do if she caught us eavesdropping?"

"It's too ugly to imagine," Haley said melodramatically.

"So now what?" Nikki asked.

"Is there a light in here?" Danielle asked. She felt the wall near the door, and found the switch. "There. That's better," she said when the light came on.

"Maybe we can hear something through the wall," Tori whispered. She pressed her ear to the wall that Kathy's office shared with the supply closet. "I can hear her voice, but I can't make out the words."

"Let's try the glass trick," Haley said. "I have a magic book that says if you take an empty glass and hold it against a wall, it'll magnify the sound. Morgan and

I tried it, and it really works." The girls searched the shelves for a glass. There were bandages, ice packs, a heating pad, boot laces, stacks of business forms, boxes of pens and pencils, and office supplies, but no sign of a glass.

"Would these work?" asked Nikki, holding up a stack of paper cups.

"No. It has to be glass," Haley said.

"What about this?" Tori asked, pointing to an empty glass jar.

"Perfect," Haley said.

She took the jar, held it to the wall, and pressed her ear against the bottom of it. The voice sounded louder, but the words were still muffled. She shook her head. "I hear her talking but can't make anything out."

"I still don't think we should be doing this," Danielle said. "I mean, we're eavesdropping. Isn't it illegal or something?"

"No one's going to catch us. And anyway, what do you think they're going to do, arrest four kids?" Tori said.

"Yeah. And it's for a good cause. We have to find out what's going on with Kathy. Let me try it," Nikki said, reaching for the glass. She put her ear to the jar.

"Anything?" Tori asked impatiently.

Nikki shook her head. "Almost, but not quite. Maybe a different spot." She moved the glass around. "Wait. I think I'm getting something. She's saying—"

At that moment the door swung open.

The four girls spun around. Nikki dropped the jar. It hit the floor with a loud crash, and shattered.

Ernie Harper, the weight trainer, stood in the doorway, staring at them in surprise. He ran a hand through his short, curly hair, the muscles in his arm bulging.

"Well, fancy meeting you here. What are you girls doing?" he asked them.

"Umm, actually, we were just looking for a bandage, Ernie," Haley said, thinking quickly.

"What's going on out there?" Kathy called from inside her office.

Haley's heart sank. In a second Kathy would come out and then they'd be in real trouble—again.

"Everything's fine," Haley quickly shouted. "Tori just cut her finger, is all."

"I'll take care of it," Ernie yelled to Kathy. To Tori he said, "I hope it's nothing serious."

Haley responded for her friend. "No, no. It's just a tiny, little cut. Nothing serious at all. We're sorry about the jar. It just slipped off the shelf. I'll get a broom and sweep it up," she babbled.

"I'll sweep it up," Ernie said. "We don't want anyone else getting hurt. Now then, a bandage." He rummaged in the first aid kit and found a box of bandages. "Here we are," he said, holding one out to Tori. "Better let me take a look at that cut. It might be worse than you think."

Tori snatched the bandage. "Thanks, Ernie, but it's

much better now. It's fine. It doesn't hurt at all."

"And we've got to go. We're late. Sorry about the jar, Ernie," Nikki cried.

The four girls rushed out of the supply closet and ran straight to the locker room, where they collapsed on the benches in fits of laughter.

"You should have seen your face when Ernie opened that door!" Haley said to Danielle. "I've never seen anyone look so scared in my life."

"My face? What about yours when Kathy called out. I thought you were going to lose it," Danielle replied.

"We're just lucky Ernie found us. He's so nice. He never gets angry about anything. If Kathy had come out . . ." Tori's voice trailed off.

"She would know we were up to something. It's one thing to fool Ernie, but another to fool Kathy," Nikki said with a grin.

"At least our mission was successful," Tori said. "What did you hear, Nikki?" Nikki's grin faded. "She said, 'I can't wait to tour with you. Only four weeks to go.' "

"I really think she's leaving to join the Ice Follies with Amy," Haley said.

"What else could she mean about going on tour?" Nikki asked.

No one had an answer.

Tori broke the silence. "Judging by the way she reacted to your little joke on Monday, I'd say it's pretty obvious that something's up."

"What do you mean?" Haley asked.

"I mean the way she went berserk over the laugh box. It's obvious she's sick of us," said Tori. "To her we're probably just a bunch of bratty kids. She probably figures, why should I stay here, when they don't even appreciate what I try to do for them."

Haley's eyes widened. Was Tori right? Did Kathy really feel that way? Did she really think they didn't appreciate her? Maybe a lot of this was Haley's own fault. After all, she was the one who always clowned around and played jokes. Haley's stomach twisted into a knot. "B-but, I told her I didn't mean to do it," she said.

"This time you did, but what about all the other times? Maybe she's just had it," Tori said.

"But Kathy knows how we feel about her," Danielle said.

"Does she?" asked Tori.

"Well, if she doesn't, we'll just have to show her," Nikki said. "And change her mind about leaving."

"Do you think we can convince her?" Haley asked doubtfully.

"Hey, Kathy said four weeks, so we've got one whole month to change her mind," Danielle said.

"That should definitely give us enough time," Nikki added.

6

Haley zapped Tori's, Nikki's, and Danielle's burgers in the microwave at the snack bar.

"You're here alone today? Where's Harry?" Jordan McShane asked when he, Alex Beekman, and Kyle Dorset saw her behind the counter.

"He had to run an errand. He'll be back soon. So decide what you want to eat while I fix some sandwiches," Haley said, wiping her hands on her apron and picking up her order pad.

It was Saturday. Two more weeks until Patrick's party. Two and a half until he got his cast off. And only three and a half weeks to persuade Kathy to stay. But Haley didn't want to start worrying about that all over again. She had to be alert on the job. All this week Haley had worked with either Timmy or Harry. They had done the grilling, but she had done everything else. She pretty much had the hang of the job, although she worked for only one hour each afternoon. Today, though, she had the lunch shift with Harry, and, she had to admit, it was harder than it looked. Much harder. She hoped he'd get back soon.

"Hmm," Jordan debated. "Should I risk something cooked by Haley?" he teased.

"I don't know. Knowing Haley and her jokes, I'd check it out carefully before I ate it," Kyle answered, grinning.

"Oh, come on. I'm not that bad," said Haley. "But you'll have to have microwaved burgers because Harry doesn't want me working the grill alone yet."

"Harry knows what he's doing," Kyle kidded. "I just wish I'd been there the other day when you set the laugh box off in the middle of Kathy's speech."

Haley blushed. Great, she thought. The whole hockey team knows about it. "Look, it was a mistake, okay? Let's just drop it. Kathy's already angry enough about it."

"I know. I heard her telling our hockey coach that her skaters are really out of control lately," Kyle said, still laughing.

"Yeah, but your coach should be used to it by now," Alex teased him. "You guys are always out of control."

Haley didn't laugh. "Did Kathy really say that?" she asked. Maybe Tori was right. Maybe Kathy really was sick of them, she thought.

"Something like that," Kyle said with a shrug. "I'll have a burger and fries."

"Same. With everything on the burger. Plus a large Coke," said Jordan.

"Make mine a cheeseburger," said Kyle.

"I'll have pizza and an orange juice," said Alex.

As she finished taking their order, four more guys from the hockey team came in and sat down in one of the booths. Haley recognized them from the rink, but she didn't know their names. She was trying to decide whether to take their order first or zap the burgers in the microwave, when she remembered the burgers for Nikki, Danielle, and Tori that were still in there. She dashed back to the microwave, opened it, and rotated the burgers. She checked the fries in the deep fryer, prepared two more burgers for the microwave, and put a slice of pizza in the oven. Then she poured three Cokes and gave them to Alex, Kyle, and Jordan.

"Hey! I ordered a large Coke," Kyle complained.

"Me too," said Jordan.

"Oh, right. Sorry." She whisked the drinks away, raced back to the drink machine, poured three large Cokes, and put them in front of the boys. Beads of sweat were starting to form on her forehead.

"Uh, I didn't order a Coke. I had an orange juice," Alex reminded her.

"Oh, yeah." Haley whisked the Coke away, poured the orange juice, and placed it in front of Kyle.

"No, the OJ's for me, not Kyle," said Alex. "Some waitress you are."

Haley ignored his comment and set the juice in front of Alex. Then she grabbed the order pad and ran to take the order from the new table.

In her mind she went over everything she had learned that week. Write down the orders one at a time. Start the cooked items, serve the drinks, then make the sandwiches. Chips, candy, and cookies are self-service, but don't forget to add them to the total. She took a deep breath and said, "Ready to order?"

"Yeah. I'm ready," said a skinny guy with hair cut really short on the sides and spiked up on top. He had an earring in one earlobe. Haley knew he was in the eighth grade and a friend of Danielle's older brother, Nicholas. She had heard that he was a good hockey player, but she still couldn't remember his name.

"I'll have a burger, I guess. No, actually make that a chicken salad sandwich and a Sprite," the guy said.

The others couldn't make up their minds, so Haley started to walk away. "I've got to check the microwave," she called back to them. "I'll be right back."

"Wait. Just give me a burger and fries," one of the guys yelled.

"Me too," said another.

"And I'll have two slices of pizza," said the third.

"Drinks?" asked Haley, furiously writing down their orders.

They gave her their drink orders and Haley rushed to the microwave. The burgers for Nikki, Danielle, and Tori looked really dried out, but Haley decided they were okay. She put them on plates with lettuce and tomato, set Kyle's and Jordan's in the microwave, and served her friends.

Tori looked at hers. "Gee, it looks kind of gray."

"It's a little overcooked," snapped Haley. "So I'm not Superchef. This isn't a fancy restaurant either. Please, just eat it. I'm way behind here." Where was Harry? she wondered, feeling panicked.

Nikki shrugged. "Let's give her a break," she said. She took a bite of her burger, made a face, and then put on a fake smile. "Delicious."

"Yeah, so delicious that I'm . . ." Tori finished her sentence by pretending to gag. Nikki and Danielle laughed.

Haley wasn't amused. "Look, I'm doing the best I can," she said, her voice rising. "Harry's supposed to be here, and it's not my fault that he's not."

"I'm just kidding. Don't get so mad," Tori said.

"Yeah, well, you should try this sometime. It's not so easy!" Haley wondered how Patrick managed. She never realized how hard he worked.

Kyle and Alex started yelling for their food, so Haley hurried back to the microwave. This time the burgers looked a little underdone, but that was okay, she decided. They'd have to do. She slapped the hamburgers on plates and grabbed the pizza from the oven. It still felt a little cold. She hoped Alex wouldn't notice.

But the minute she put down his plate he felt the pizza. "Haley! This is still frozen," he cried. "I can't eat it like this. Can you heat it up some more?" Haley sighed and took the pizza back.

"Hey," yelled Kyle. "This burger moved. It's still alive! Did you cook it at all?"

"Most people like them rare," Haley replied.

"Rare, maybe, but not raw."

She took their food and put it back in the microwave, and then started preparing the other hockey players' order. She dashed madly from the microwave to the counter to the booths, and no matter how hard she tried, it seemed she couldn't keep the orders straight.

She was just about to serve the hockey players, when Kathy and Mr. Weiler walked in and sat at the counter. Oh, great, she thought. Just what I need.

"I'll be right there to take your order," she called as she rushed passed them with a tray of food.

"Hey, you forgot my cheese," yelled one of the hockey players.

"Where's the ketchup?" shouted another.

"Just a minute," Haley said. She hurried back to their table and tried to fix their order.

"When's Patrick coming back?" one of them asked.

"Yeah. We want Patrick! We want Patrick!" they chanted.

"Don't let those clowns bother you," said Kathy. "You're doing fine. It's a zoo in here on weekends. It was really sweet of you to offer to help Patrick out."

"Thanks," Haley said, proud that Kathy had complimented her. "But I didn't know it was going to be so crazy."

"Where's Harry?" Mr. Weiler asked.

"He said he'd be right back. You ready to order?"

She wrote down their order and then turned to the sandwich counter to make it. Kathy and Mr. Weiler continued talking, and as she worked, Haley heard some of their conversation.

"Are you sure about this?" Mr. Weiler said seriously.

"Well, almost," Kathy replied. "Besides, this is something I've always wanted to do. I told Amy I'd do it, and I don't want to let her down."

Mr. Weiler sighed. "Well, I suppose we'll manage to survive without you."

"And Anita will be great for the kids. It's not finalized yet, but I really think they'd be better off . . ." She glanced at Haley, who pretended not to notice, and lowered her voice.

So it was true, Haley thought. It was really true! Kathy was going to leave them. She was going to leave them and join the Ice Follies!

7

"**H**aley! Wait up," Patrick called.

Haley's shift at the snack bar was finally over, and she was hurrying to find Nikki, Tori, and Danielle. They'd left before she had a chance to tell them what Kathy and Mr. Weiler had said.

"Patrick, hi," she said, waiting for him to catch up to her. "You're getting a lot better with the crutches."

"Yeah, but I still hate them," he said. "How's it going in the snack bar?"

"Not so great. It was crazy today. You always made it look so easy."

He nodded. "It takes a while to get the hang of it. When I first started I could never keep the orders straight. And I kept burning things."

Haley smiled. "You just described my shift."

"Yeah, but you'll get used to it," he assured her.

"I guess so," she said. "What have you been doing?"

"Lifting weights and swimming laps. I want to do everything I can to stay in shape while my ankle heals."

"Great. You'll be ready for Regionals," Haley pointed out.

"I don't know," Patrick said.

The doubt in his voice made Haley realize that his fall had also affected his confidence. "But we've definitely got a shot at a medal," she said.

"We did," he said.

"We still do," Haley insisted.

"Well, whatever," Patrick replied.

"Hey, partner, we're the best," Haley said. She stuck her hand out and they slapped, once, twice, and then a high five. For the first time since the accident, Haley saw him crack a real smile.

She wondered if she should tell Patrick about Kathy, but decided against it. After all, she was pretty sure they could persuade her to stay. Besides, she didn't want to give Patrick another thing to worry about.

"Haley, listen, you really saved my life by taking my job at the snack bar. Thanks a lot," Patrick said.

"Hey, anything for my partner," Haley said. It felt good to help Patrick out—even if it *was* killing her.

"Well, back to the weight room. I'll see you later," he said, and he hobbled off down the hall.

That night Tori, Nikki, and Danielle gathered at Haley's house for a sleepover. Since the next day was Sunday, they didn't have to get up for practice. Tori was curled up on Haley's pillow, Haley lay on her stomach across the bottom of the bed, Nikki sat cross-legged on the floor, a bowl of popcorn beside her, and Danielle was stretched out on her sleeping bag. They discussed what Haley had overheard in the snack bar that afternoon.

"Mr. Weiler actually said, 'We'll manage to survive without you'? I mean, were those his exact words?" asked Tori.

"His exact words, I swear it," said Haley.

"But Kathy didn't say she was one hundred percent sure she's leaving. She only said she's *almost* sure, right?" Nikki pointed out.

"But did she also say, 'I told Amy I'd do it, and I don't want to let her down'?" Danielle asked.

Haley nodded. "We've been over this about twenty times."

"You better hope she changes her mind," Tori said. "Because if she doesn't, you and Patrick won't be going to the Regionals, even if Patrick's ankle is better."

"What are you talking about?" Haley snapped.

Tori shrugged. "You don't have to believe me, but it's true. I was talking to Diana Mitchell," Tori said.

"What does she know about it?" Haley asked. Diana was sixteen and a Silver Blades skater longer than anyone else, but she didn't know everything, Haley thought.

"She said there's no way a new coach would let you go," Tori said. "And she heard Mr. Weiler telling Kathy he didn't think Patrick should go because he shouldn't put that much stress on his ankle so soon."

"Patrick's in better shape than he was before he hurt his ankle," Haley cried. "He swims and works out every day."

"But he hasn't worked out his ankle," Tori pointed out. "Anyway, it's not the end of the world. It's just one competition. There'll be others."

Just one competition! How could Tori say that. "You know how important this competition is to us, Tori," Haley cried.

"Haley and Patrick have a good chance at a medal," Nikki said. "They've got to go."

Tori shrugged. "All I know is what I heard." She stood up and walked over to Haley's bureau, where she picked up a brush and started to run it through her hair. "You don't have to bite my head off, Haley. Anyway, maybe Kathy did get sick of all your practical jokes."

Haley looked down, biting her lip. Was it true? Was she the reason Kathy was leaving?

"Tori! That's not true, and you know it," Danielle said quickly. "If Kathy's leaving, it's probably because she's tired of coaching and wants to perform professionally. It has nothing to do with Haley."

Haley shot Danielle a grateful look. "But if she does feel unappreciated," Haley said, "maybe we can change her mind. Maybe we can show her how much we care about her, and how much we need her."

"How do we do that?" Nikki asked.

"Let's see. We need a plan," Haley said, sitting up.

"We could start by getting her a card. Like a thank-you card for what a good coach she is," Danielle said.

"That's good," Nikki said.

"Great!" said Haley.

"She did say it's not finalized yet, right?" Nikki asked. "So that means there's still time for us to change her mind. This might really work."

"It has to work," Haley told them. "Alex and Nikki and Patrick and I need Kathy. She's the best!"

The following Monday after practice, Haley, Nikki, Danielle, and Tori sat in the bleachers taking off their skates. Out on the ice, Kathy skated alone, unaware that the girls were watching her. She skated in a wide circle and then rose into a perfect double salchow.

"Wow! Did you see that?" whispered Haley.

Tori nodded. "That's why she came in fourth in the Nationals. Kathy's a great skater."

As they watched Kathy, Haley grabbed her skating bag and pulled out the card they had bought on Sunday. It said, "To a very special friend, thanks for everything." Haley had crossed off "friend" and written in "coach," then signed her name inside the card and passed it to Danielle.

"When should we give it to her?" asked Danielle as she printed her name under Haley's and passed it on to Tori.

"Let's put it on her desk and let her find it," said Nikki.

"She's still out on the ice. Let's sneak into her office now," Danielle said.

"Good idea. Come on," Haley said.

They headed for Kathy's office with the card.

The door was open so the girls walked in. "Should we put it next to Porky the Porcupine?" Danielle asked, pointing to the tiny stuffed porcupine at the edge of Kathy's desk.

"She sure has weird taste in stuffed animals," Tori said.

"No, I think the card should be near her coffee mug, since she's always drinking coffee," Haley said. She propped the card up against Kathy's mug.

"Look at this," Nikki said, pointing to a pink while-you-were-out slip on the coach's desk. The message said, "Amy called."

"Amy again," Danielle said, frowning. "I'm getting to hate her, and I've never even met her."

"She's trying to steal our coach away from us," Nikki said.

"We should go to the Ice Follies and boo her," Tori said.

"Uh-oh." Haley heard footsteps coming toward the office. "Someone's coming. Let's get out of here now."

They scrambled out of the office and almost ran into Kathy.

"Now what are you girls up to?" she asked. "Another prank?" She eyed Haley.

"No, no. We were just looking for you," said Haley.

Kathy gave them a skeptical look. "Why do I have a hard time believing that?"

"No, really," Haley insisted. "See, Nikki has a problem she needs to talk to you about. She's worried."

"I am?" Nikki asked, looking at Haley. Haley raised her eyebrows, hoping Nikki would catch on. "Oh, yes, I am," Nikki said.

"Oh?" said Kathy. "Are you worried about qualifying for the competition? Because if that's it, I don't think you have to worry. I'm certain you and Alex will pass the test and make it."

Everyone looked at Nikki. "I, uh, I'm worried because I'm not sure my parents will let me go. They don't understand how important it is."

Haley sighed with relief. Nikki usually wasn't so good at making up stories.

"Really?" said Kathy. "That sure doesn't sound like your parents, Nikki. They've always been so supportive."

"But it's close to the time the baby's due, and Mom's more worried about everything than she was a few months ago," Nikki replied.

"Well, next time I see your mother I'll talk to her about it. I'm sure I can persuade her to let you go. Don't worry. We'll work something out," Kathy promised.

The four girls followed the coach into her office. She sat down behind the desk and reached for her coffee mug. "What's this?" she said when she saw the card.

"Open it," Haley urged.

"So it *is* another one of your jokes." She opened the card, read it, and then looked at the girls, a large smile on her face. "Oh, you guys. This is really sweet." She gave each of them a hug, first Danielle, then Nikki, then Tori, and finally Haley. "And here I suspected you of evil doings."

She glanced at the card again. "But what did I do to deserve this?" she asked.

"We just wanted to get you a card," Tori said.

"We want you to know that we really do appreciate you," Haley said.

"Well, you're very sweet," said Kathy. "And now I've got work to do, so out you go."

She turned back to her desk as the girls moved toward the door. "And don't worry, Nikki. I'll be sure to talk to your mother this week."

When they were out of earshot of the office, Danielle spoke up. "Is your mother really thinking about not letting you go?" she asked Nikki.

"No, I just made that up," Nikki said. "Pretty smart, huh?"

"Well, what's your mother going to say when Kathy talks to her?" Danielle asked.

Nikki looked worried for a second. "My mom won't have a clue what Kathy's taking about. Maybe she'll think she really did say those things to me and forgot. She does forget a lot of things these days—she's always thinking about the baby." She laughed and shrugged. "Or else she'll just think I'm weird, I guess, but that's okay."

"Yeah. You are weird. She might as well know it," Haley teased.

"Yeah, look who's talking," Nikki shot back.

"You have a point," Haley said, giggling. "But you were great in there."

"And Kathy loved the card," Tori pointed out.

"It was perfect," Haley said. "Now, what's our next move?"

8

"You should see the new mare at the stables, Mom. She's beautiful. I can't wait to ride her," Morgan said. It was Friday, and the Arthurs were eating dinner at the table in the little room off the kitchen. Her mother called it the breakfast nook, but Haley thought it should be called the dinner nook, because that's where they ate evening meals. They used the dining room only when they had guests, which was fine with Haley because setting the breakfast nook was a lot easier than setting the large dining room table, and that was her job.

"Oh, I'd love to see her," Haley's mother said. "Maybe tomorrow I'll stop by and have a look."

There they go again, Haley thought. Can't they ever talk about anything besides horses? She looked at her father and rolled her eyes. He winked back. At least her father wasn't a horse fanatic.

As her mother and Morgan kept discussing the new mare, her father let out a loud whinny, something he did whenever the two of them went on about horses for too long. Haley's mother stopped talking and glared at her husband.

"Well, the only way to get any attention around here is to act like a horse," Mr. Arthur said.

"Okay, okay. We get the message. No more horse talk," said Haley's mother. She reached for the platter of meat loaf and took a small piece. "Anyone else want more?" she asked, passing the platter to Haley, who shook her head.

"You're pretty quiet tonight, Hals. Something on your mind?" her mother asked her.

"Yeah, what's up?" her father added.

These days Mr. Arthur traveled a lot because of his promotion so he always tried to get Haley to talk to him, even when she didn't feel like talking. She knew he was just trying to be a good father, but sometimes she wished he'd leave her alone.

"Not much," Haley said.

"How's Patrick doing? Does he know if he'll be able to skate in the competition?" asked her father.

"We don't know yet," she said. "He has another checkup with the doctor next week."

"Marci says she can't wait till Patrick is better so he can go back to the snack bar. She says you burn everything," Morgan said.

"Marci's a brat," Haley said. Marci Dwyer was a younger member of Silver Blades who was in Morgan's class at Kent Academy.

"Maybe it's too much for you, working at the snack bar," her mother said worriedly. "You seem tired lately."

"No, it's fine. It was hard at first, but it's better now. I'm getting the hang of it. I've already been there almost two weeks, and Patrick will probably be back in another two. And I don't burn everything. At least, not anymore."

"Well, that's what Marci said. But she's kind of dumb sometimes," Morgan said.

"There is one thing I'm worried about though," Haley said.

"What's that?" asked her father.

"We're pretty sure Kathy is leaving Silver Blades," Haley told them.

"Not Kathy Bart?" her mother asked.

Haley nodded. "She might be joining the Ice Follies," Haley said. She told her parents a little about what she had heard, carefully leaving out the part about hiding in the supply closet.

"Are you sure about this?" asked her father.

"Well, it's not definite, but . . ."

"Kathy's certainly a good enough skater to be in the Ice Follies. It's understandable that she might want to do something different while she's still young. She can always coach, but she won't always be able to skate well enough for the Follies," said her mother.

Haley couldn't believe it. Her mother sounded

almost as though she wanted Kathy to leave. Didn't she understand how important Kathy was to her?

"If she leaves, I'll die," Haley told them. "I'll quit skating. What would be the point?"

"I think you're overreacting, Haley. I know you respect Kathy, but I'm sure the club will find a replacement. There are plenty of other good coaches," her mother said.

"None as good as Kathy," Haley insisted.

"How do you know? She's the only coach you've ever had," her dad said.

"And you're always complaining about how mean and tough she is, and how she works you to death," Morgan said.

"We know it will be hard to lose her," said her father, "but it's your talent and determination that make you such a fine skater, not your coach. I'm sure another coach will be able to work with you as well."

"That's right. Remember last year when Morgan's riding instructor left? She thought it was the end of the world, and now look. She loves Ms. Blackster even more," said her mother.

There she goes again, Haley thought. Comparing everything to riding. Suddenly Haley couldn't stand it anymore. She stood up, knocking her chair back against the wall. "It's not the same. It's not the same at all," she shouted, as she ran out of the room and raced upstairs.

Haley slammed her bedroom door shut, clicked the lock, and flopped down on her bed. She was angry, but she wouldn't let herself cry.

She found the crack in the ceiling and stared at it. It had been there all her life, never getting bigger or smaller. The crack looked like the profile of her second-grade teacher, Ms. Harvey, complete with her huge nose and her jutting chin. Haley could hear Ms. Harvey talking to her now. "You're in second grade, Haley. Second graders are too old to cry over a little problem."

"Okay, Ms. Harvey, okay. I know I'm too old to cry, but I just wish my mother could understand a few things," she said aloud. Like, why couldn't her mother see that skating meant everything to her? And why did her mother always have to say, "Something like that happened to Morgan," or "When that happens at the stables . . ."

Of course that was because her mother was always at the stables, never at the skating rink with Haley. And because her mother loved horses. But couldn't she see that their situations were totally different? First of all, Morgan was almost two years younger than Haley. And second, she wasn't in a special program like Silver Blades. Skating was everything to Haley, but riding was just a hobby to Morgan. Her mother just couldn't see the difference. She'll never understand how important my coach is to me. A lot more important than Morgan's stupid riding instructor!

Haley picked up the photo of Kathy hugging her after she won a gold medal in the Novice Regionals. She stared at the picture, thinking about all the things she went through with Kathy, all the times the coach encouraged her or comforted her. Sure, she was tough, but that was fair. That's part of what made her a good coach. But most of all, Kathy was always there. Especially for Haley. And now, with Kathy possibly leaving, Haley didn't know what she would do.

There was a knock on her door. "Go away," said Haley.

"It's Morgan. Can I come in?"

Haley sighed, but she went to the door and unlocked it. Then she flopped back down on her bed.

Morgan came in and perched on the arm of Haley's chair. She picked up a stuffed gray cat and stroked its fur.

"Why'd you get so mad at dinner?" she asked.

Haley frowned. "Mom doesn't understand anything about skating. I'm sick of her always comparing it to riding. I bet she wishes I rode too."

"No, she doesn't," said Morgan.

"How do you know?" Haley asked.

"Because I heard her talking to Mrs. Diaz." The Diazes had moved next door to the Arthurs a few weeks before. "Mrs. Diaz asked why you have to get up so early, and Mom told her about your skating," Morgan said.

"Yeah, so?"

"Well, Mrs. Diaz said, 'You must be very proud of her.' And Mom said, 'Oh, I am. Sometimes I can hardly believe it's my own daughter out there on the ice. She just amazes me.'"

Haley sat up and looked at Morgan to make sure she was telling the truth. "She really said that?"

Morgan nodded.

"Well, she probably didn't mean it. If she's so proud, why doesn't she ever come to practice to watch me skate. How come she's always at the stables with you?"

Morgan shrugged. "I don't know. Why don't you ask her?" She hopped off the chair and sat down on the bed next to Haley. "Is Kathy really leaving Silver Blades?" she asked, glancing at the picture Haley was holding.

"I sure hope not," Haley said.

"Me too," Morgan said.

"How come? You hardly even know her," Haley said.

"But I don't want you to quit skating," Morgan told her.

9

The next day, Saturday, Haley was working hard on her jumps, when she saw Patrick watching her from the stands. She waved and skated over to the barrier, ready for a break.

"Your axel is looking good. You've really improved it," he said.

"Thanks. Now I have to land the double. I guess it's good I had some time to concentrate on it alone. If I nail it, we can add it to our program." She leaned on the barrier and slid her skates back and forth on the ice. "So what did the doctor say? How much longer?" she asked him.

"Eleven more days," he said with a sigh. "I'm really getting sick of this. I can't wait to get back on skates."

"Well, that did not even two weeks," Haley said, trying to sound encouraging.

"Except that a week seems like a year when you just sit here watching everyone else skate," Patrick complained. When he wasn't swimming or working with Ernie, Patrick often sat in the bleachers watching the other skaters. He said he hated to be away from the rink.

"It must be awful," Haley agreed. She had never seen him so miserable before. She sure hoped that the party would cheer him up, but it wasn't until the next Saturday. She wished they'd been able to have it earlier.

"Hey, you want to do something later?" he asked, tapping his crutches against the barrier. "Go to the arcade in the mall and play some games or something?"

Haley panicked. She was supposed to meet her friends and Alex, Kyle, and Jordan at Super Sundaes to talk about Patrick's party, but she couldn't tell him *that*.

"I can't," she said, quickly making up an excuse. "Morgan's got a horse show, and I've got to go. My parents are making me."

"Oh. Okay." He sounded so down that Haley felt awful.

"Maybe we could go to the arcade tomorrow though," she suggested. She and Patrick often hung out there together. They both loved video games.

"Great!" he said, sounding a little happier.

Later that afternoon, after another crazy lunchtime shift at the snack bar, Haley met her friends at Super Sundaes. They all were squeezed into one of the big booths that held eight people. Haley couldn't even think of eating after staring at all the snack bar food, but everyone else ordered regular sundaes, except for Alex, who ordered the super special, five scoops of ice cream with five different toppings.

"I can't believe you're really going to eat all that," Danielle said to Alex.

"Peanut butter ice cream with strawberry topping? That's disgusting," Tori said.

"What's wrong with it?" asked Alex. "You have peanut butter and jelly sandwiches, don't you?"

"Yeah, but not with my ice cream sundaes," said Kyle.

"Well, you guys don't have to eat it," Alex said, dishing himself an enormous spoonful of ice cream.

"But we have to watch *you* eat it!" Jordan teased.

Nikki held up a hand. "Okay. Let him eat his disgusting sundae. We've got to talk about Patrick's surprise party. Harry agreed to have it at the snack bar. Does everyone know about it? Is there anyone else we need to invite?"

"Everyone in Silver Blades knows. How about anyone else from the hockey team?" Haley asked.

"You told Nicholas, right, Danielle? And I invited Tom Steiner," said Kyle. "Is there anyone else?"

"They're the only guys from the team that Patrick is good friends with. Besides us," Jordan said.

"And I don't know any of the kids he goes to school with."

"I think we've got it covered, then," Alex said.

"Okay," said Haley, taking out her school notebook and a pen. "I'll order the pizzas. Can someone bring some chips and stuff? And what about drinks?"

"Each of us should bring two of those big two-liter bottles of soda," Danielle suggested. "That's fourteen bottles. That ought to do it."

They listed everything else they needed for the party, and Haley wrote it all down. "Okay," she said, reviewing her list. "I think we're in good shape. I just hope this party cheers him up."

"Well, if it doesn't, then nothing will," Jordan said.

"He'll be fine as soon as he gets back on the ice," Alex said.

"He has only eleven more days to go," Haley said.

"Hey, look who's here," Kyle said, nodding toward the door. He put his thumb and finger in his mouth and whistled. "Patrick. Over here."

When Patrick saw them, he waved and headed toward their booth, moving slowly with his crutches.

"Oh, no," Haley whispered.

"What?" Danielle asked.

"He asked me if I wanted to do something earlier, and I told him I had to go to Morgan's horse show. I didn't want to tell him we were meeting because of the party. Now what am I going to say?" Haley whispered.

"Here he comes. Wing it," Danielle whispered back, smiling at Patrick.

Patrick stood beside their booth. The others began to squeeze in to make room for him.

"Hey, what's this? A party? Thanks for inviting me."

"Why would we invite you? Do you think we like to torture ourselves?" Alex joked.

"Move over, fatso." Patrick punched Kyle lightly on the arm.

Then he spotted Haley. His smile faded and for a minute he said nothing. Haley knew what he was thinking. She felt like sliding under the table and disappearing. "Haley? What are you doing here?" he finally said. "I thought you had to go to a horse show."

"Umm, I did. It, uh, it was canceled at the last minute. They do that sometimes, you know. Sometimes the horses don't feel well or something. I don't why, but . . . anyway . . . they do and it was canceled and . . . here I am." Haley knew she was babbling, but she couldn't seem to stop. She could see that Patrick didn't believe her. She hated lying to him—but she couldn't ruin the surprise. "Patrick—" she started up again.

"Look, just forget it. There's no law that says you have to hang out with your skating partner. Especially one who can't skate."

With that he turned and hobbled off.

"Patrick!" Haley shouted after him, but he didn't turn around. She felt awful.

"Whoa!" Nikki cried. "He's really upset. Maybe we should just tell him about the party."

"No. That would wreck everything. It has to be a surprise. The party's only a week away," said Tori.

"But I've got to do something," Haley said. She jumped out of the booth and dashed after Patrick.

"Patrick, wait up. Please don't be mad. I—"

"Why should I be mad?" he said, cutting her off and stopping in his tracks. "I mean, I'm left out of skating, and now you leave me out of your plans altogether. Well, why don't you just leave me alone from now on? Just forget I exist." He turned and limped off, leaving Haley feeling worse than she ever had in her life.

She slowly rejoined her friends. "I'll be lucky if he even wants to skate with me after this," she said.

"Once we have the surprise party, he'll understand. I guarantee it," Tori reassured her.

"I suppose so," said Haley, still feeling pretty bad.

When everyone finished their sundaes, the girls went to Sports Sensations at the other end of the mall to look at the new line of skates.

"These are incredible," Tori said, eyeing the display. "I'm going to try them. If they fit, I'll get a pair."

"You just got a new pair of skates, Tori," Danielle reminded her.

"I know, but these are really fantastic. Feel this boot. The leather is so soft, but it has great support," Tori said.

Haley shook her head. "Pretty soon you'll have a pair of skates to go with every skating dress you have, Tori."

"I doubt that, since I have over fifteen skating dresses," Tori said.

Haley, Nikki, and Danielle just looked at one another and laughed. There was no doubt about it. Tori was a fashion queen just like her mom, who was a top fashion designer. Tori would never change.

"Hey, look at these. They're so cool," Nikki cried, pointing at a group of stuffed animals on ice skates arranged on the gift table. Nikki held up a little stuffed elephant wearing a purple skating dress, posed in a spin.

"I love it!" cried Danielle. "Look at this one." She picked up a rabbit in a green body suit. The rabbit's ears stuck straight out behind him, like a speed skater's.

"Oh, look at this," Haley exclaimed. She picked up a hedgehog wearing sunglasses, a leather jacket, and ice skates.

"We've got to get this for Kathy. She loves weird stuffed animals," Nikki said.

"Right. Part of our plan to show her we need her," Tori added.

"What do you think, Haley? Should we get it for Kathy?" Nikki asked.

"Definitely. She'll love it," Haley said. "And Porky the Porcupine on her desk will have a pairs partner."

"Well, I hope this works," Nikki said.

"If it doesn't, we've still got some time to work on her, right?" Tori said. "I mean, she isn't going until the day after the Regionals."

"But that's not even two weeks away," Haley noted.

They paid for the little animal and left the store. As they walked through the mall, Nikki nudged Haley. "You're pretty quiet," she said. "Still worried about Patrick?"

Haley nodded. "I feel so stupid. Why did I have to make up that dumb lie about the horse show? Now he'll never trust me again."

"He'll get over it. Especially when he finds out about the party next Saturday," said Nikki.

"I know," said Haley. She sure hoped the week would pass quickly.

10

Haley arrived at the rink earlier than usual Monday morning. She had the ice all to herself, and as she warmed up in the quiet dimness of the half-lit rink, she thought about how she loved the morning skate. It was hard having to get up at four-thirty every day, but once she was up, it was worth it.

As she skated she felt every muscle in her body responding to the ice, and she was ready to spin and jump for the sheer joy of being on skates. She felt so good, as if she could do anything, and suddenly, almost before she knew what happened, she was springing into the air from the outside edge of her left skate and spinning, once, twice, and a final half rotation before she landed on her right edge. She did it! She landed a double axel!

I have to tell Kathy, she thought. Then she heard

clapping coming from the bleachers. She looked up, and there was Kathy sitting in the stands watching her.

Haley skated over to the edge of the rink. "I did it!" she shouted. "Did you see me?"

"I saw you. It was beautiful! Congratulations. I knew you'd get it any day now." Kathy stood up and came down out of the stands.

Other skaters started to arrive. They put on their skates and headed out onto the ice. Kathy walked to the far wall and snapped on the rest of the lights.

Haley saw Nikki and Danielle and called to them. "Guess what—I landed a double axel!"

"You're kidding!" shouted Nikki. "That's great. When?"

"Just now. I got here early and was warming up, and before I knew what I was doing I landed it. I didn't even think about it." Haley was so excited—her heart beat double time. "I wish Patrick had seen it." Even though he was mad at her, she knew he'd still be very happy for her.

"Wow. A double axel. Now you, Jill, and Tori can all do one," said Nikki. She put her arm around Danielle's shoulders. "I guess that leaves the two of us. We'd better get to work."

"You'll land yours soon," Haley said. "If I can do it, you guys can."

Danielle opened her skating bag. "Here's our stuffed hedgehog," she said. "When should we give it to Kathy?"

"Her clipboard is sitting right there," Haley said, pointing to a seat in the bleachers. "What if we just put it on top of it and let her find it. She'll be back to pick it up any minute now."

"Good idea," said Danielle. They headed to the clipboard and Danielle set the hedgehog on top of it. "There's Tori. Just in time."

They called Tori over, then stood nearby, waiting for Kathy.

"Shh. Here she comes," Tori said.

Kathy hurried toward the girls. "All right, everybody," she shouted. "Time to get to work. Now!" She reached for her clipboard and saw the hedgehog. "Oh. What's this?" She picked it up and smiled. "How cute! Whose is he?"

"He's yours," Haley said.

"Okay. What's going on? Another trick or something?" Kathy demanded. She looked from one girl to the other.

"He's for you," Nikki insisted.

"We bought him yesterday," said Haley. "We figured you'd like him . . ."

"For me? But why? It's not my birthday or anything," Kathy said.

The girls shrugged. "So the porcupine in your office won't be lonely anymore," Danielle said.

"We all fell in love with him, and then we decided to buy him for you," Haley explained.

Kathy squeezed the hedgehog. "Well, I love him too. I must say, I don't know what I did to deserve him, but . . . thanks." She put her arms around all of them and gave them a joint hug.

Haley felt sure their plan to get Kathy to stay was working.

"But just because you guys are being so nice to me lately doesn't mean anything's going to change around here," Kathy said. "So out on the ice now!"

The girls stepped onto the ice and circled the rink together, warming up. "I think it's working," Tori whispered.

"I think so too," Haley said. "Did you hear what she said about how nothing's going to change around here? If nothing's going to change, maybe she isn't planning to leave anymore, right?"

"Right," Tori said.

"Let's keep it up," Haley said. "By the time we finish, she'll never be able to leave. She'll miss us too much."

"What else can we do?" asked Nikki.

"How about baking some cookies?" Haley suggested.

"Great idea! Kathy always keeps butterscotch candies on her desk. She loves them. I've got a recipe for butterscotch cookies," Tori said.

Haley nodded. "Perfect. Let's make them tonight."

"I've got a history test tomorrow," Nikki said. "I can't."

"Same here," Danielle said.

"Well, Tori and I can make them, and we can all give them to her tomorrow," Haley offered.

"Okay. You come home with me after practice this afternoon and we'll bake them," Tori said.

As Haley turned to work some more on her double axel, she felt great. Their plan was working, she was sure of it. She glanced toward the stands to see if Kathy was watching her, and her heart sank. Standing beside her coach was the same woman who'd watched them all week.

The woman was no scout, Haley was sure. She observed the skaters the way a coach would. Haley hoped that she wasn't the coach who wanted to take Kathy's place.

"We can each have one, and one only," Haley said the next day before practice as she showed Danielle and Nikki the tin of butterscotch cookies that she and Tori had baked the night before.

Danielle took a cookie and bit into it. "Mmm. These are great. Kathy will love them."

"Yum," Nikki agreed, tasting hers. "I don't know. Maybe we're overdoing it. Maybe we should keep the cookies for ourselves. After all, we don't want to go too far with all this."

"You just want the cookies," Haley said. "You can get the recipe from Tori and bake more tonight if you want, but these we're giving to Kathy."

"You're right," Danielle said. "Let's give them now before I eat the rest."

"Don't even think of it," Haley said, hugging the tin of cookies to her chest.

"Let's put them in her office and let her find them," Danielle suggested.

"Okay. Let's hurry," Tori said. "Coming late to practice sure won't help our cause."

The door to Kathy's office was ajar, so the girls sneaked in and left the tin of cookies on her desk, right beside her butterscotch candies.

"Will she know who they're from?" Nikki asked.

"Will she know who what's from?" asked Kathy as she came in the door. She looked at the tin on her desk. "What's this? Not another present?" She opened the tin and saw the cookies. "Wow. These look great." She picked one out and took a bite. "Mmm. They are great. I love butterscotch."

"We know," said Danielle.

"But what's going on? You've been showering me with gifts. I'm beginning to get suspicious here. There must be some reason."

"We just want you to know we appreciate you," Nikki said.

"Well, if I didn't know it before, I sure do now." She offered the tin of cookies around. Danielle reached for one, but Haley shot her a warning look.

"We already had some," Tori said. "Those are for you."

"Well, I'll leave them here. Help yourselves later if you get hungry. Now I've got a few phone calls to make before lessons. So, out on the ice for all of you," Kathy said. "And thanks. It is nice to feel appreciated. And

Porky is very pleased with his new friend." She pointed to the desk where her stuffed porcupine stood next to the hedgehog the girls had given her.

As the girls filed out of her office, Kathy picked up the phone. Haley hung back, and heard Kathy say, "Amy?"

Haley knew she shouldn't listen, but she couldn't resist. She stopped and stood out of sight and listened through the partially opened door.

"You'll be in on Friday?" Kathy said. "Great. I can't wait to see you and iron out the details of our plans. You'll have to tell me everything about the Ice Follies. Are you free for dinner that night?" There was a pause, and then Haley heard, "Okay. How about Giovanni's at seven?" Pause. "Terrific. I'll see you then."

Haley dashed down the hall and caught up with the others. "Guess what I just heard?" she said, repeating Kathy's conversation.

"You're sure she was talking to Amy?" Danielle asked.

"Positive. She said her name when she first made the call. That's why I stopped to listen."

"Friday night at seven?" Nikki said thoughtfully. "I say we meet there and spy on her. That way we can figure out once and for all what's going on."

"Spy on them?" Danielle said. "But what if we get caught? Can you imagine how embarrassing it would be?"

"How can we get caught? We'll just say we're

meeting our parents there or something," said Nikki.

"Friday at seven at Giovanni's," Haley said. She put her hand out and the others put theirs on top and they shook on it.

11

As she worked behind the counter at the snack bar on Thursday afternoon, Haley wondered how Patrick was doing. She hadn't seen him since the past Saturday at Super Sundaes, when he stormed out. She had called him several times, but the answering machine picked up and he never called her back. He didn't even know that she landed the double axel. And now that he didn't seem to be speaking to her, Haley wasn't sure how she'd get him to come to the party.

Still, Haley was hopeful. So when Sara Russell and Christine Rosenblum came in, she reminded them about it.

"Oh, yeah. The party on Saturday. What time?" Sara asked.

"Six o'clock. Everyone needs to be on time because it's a surprise."

"I'll be there," Christine said. "It should be a good party."

At that moment Patrick walked up to the snack bar. Uh-oh, thought Haley.

"A party?" Patrick said to Sara and Christine, pointedly ignoring her. "Whose party? When and where?"

Sara and Christine looked at Haley. For a minute no one spoke. "It's a party for someone at Kent," Haley announced quickly. "No one you know."

Patrick's smile faded. "Oh. Well, sorry. Didn't mean to butt in." He grabbed a bag of chips from the rack and threw two quarters on the counter. "See you," he said to Sara and Christine.

He left without saying anything to Haley. "Patrick, wait," Haley yelled after him. "I've been trying to call you. Did you get my messages?"

Either Patrick didn't hear or he pretended not to, because he just kept on walking.

Haley shook her head. "I feel like I should just tell him the truth," she said as she set an orange juice in front of Christine. "By the time this party gets here, he's going to be so mad at me he'll never speak to me again."

"Don't worry. Once he realizes why you've been secretive he won't be angry anymore," Christine assured her.

"I hope not, 'cause he sure is mad now."

Haley looked up to see Kathy coming into the snack bar with the mysterious woman. They sat at a table near the counter.

As she fixed some sandwiches, Haley tried to hear what they were saying. She couldn't make out everything, but she did hear the names of some of the Silver Blades skaters. And now Haley was sure of what she had only suspected before. The woman was Kathy's replacement.

The last thing Haley felt like doing was taking the woman's order. But she didn't have a choice. When she got to the table, Kathy introduced her. "Haley, this is Anita Skein. Anita, this is Haley Arthur," Kathy said. "She skates pairs with Patrick McGuire. She just landed her double axel on Monday."

"Oh, how wonderful. I saw you skating a few days ago. You have lovely form," said Anita.

"Thanks. Are you, um . . . here for any special reason?" Haley asked, hoping to get some more information but not wanting to seem rude.

"I'm just observing. I used to coach at a rink in Connecticut, but I've moved down here now, and I'm just getting to know the area."

"Oh. Will you be coaching at Silver Blades?" Haley asked.

"Haley, you'd better take our order. Looks like things are pretty busy," Kathy said, not giving Anita a chance to answer. She nodded toward the mob of kids at the counter.

"Oh, right. What can I get you?"

"I'll have the turkey sandwich on whole wheat. How about you, Anita?"

"I'll just have a salad, please, Haley," Anita said with a smile.

"Okay. I'll be right back."

While Haley made Kathy's sandwich, she replayed in her mind what Anita had said.

She was a coach, and she had just moved to this area. In other words, she was a perfect replacement for Kathy.

Haley put the sandwich and the salad on a tray and hurried back to the table. She didn't watch where she was going, and just as she reached the table she tripped and stumbled. The food flew off the tray and Kathy's sandwich landed with a plop in Anita's lap.

"Oh, no! I'm really, really sorry," Haley said as Anita picked bits of lettuce, tomato, and turkey off her lap. "Here, let me get you some more napkins."

Harry saw the whole thing and came around the counter toward them.

"I'm so sorry, miss," he said.

"I'm fine," Anita assured him. "No harm done. These things happen."

"I guess your grace on the ice doesn't extend to the snack bar, does it, Haley?" Kathy teased. She smiled at Anita. "Haley's known for her practical jokes, but I think this was an honest mistake."

"I'm really, really sorry," was all Haley could say. She had never been so embarrassed.

What a great way to start off with the new coach, she thought.

The next morning, Friday, Haley had to drag herself out of bed. She had tossed and turned all night, unable to sleep. She kept thinking about Kathy leaving and about Patrick. She tried to figure out a way to get him to come to the party without giving away the surprise. She finally gave up and decided to ask her friends for help at practice.

But that morning she was late to practice, so there was no time to talk to her friends. She felt stiff and tight on the ice. She skated around the rink several times, trying to warm up, but that fluid, comfortable feeling she usually experienced when she skated wouldn't come.

When it was time to start her lesson she knew she wouldn't be able to perform well. She tried the double axel, but today, instead of landing it perfectly as she had only four days earlier, she came down on her inside edge and stumbled, almost falling. She looked into the stands and saw Anita Skein there again, watching her closely. She must think I'm a super klutz, thought Haley. First I dump a sandwich all over her, and then I fall on my first jump.

By the end of practice Haley felt like a beginner. Nothing went right. No matter how hard she tried, she just couldn't seem to get it together.

"You look tired. Have you been getting enough sleep?" Kathy asked her.

"I didn't sleep too well last night," Haley admitted.

"Anything wrong?"

Haley hesitated. She wished she could blurt out what was bothering her. Ask Kathy if she was leaving and find out once and for all if it was true. But if she did that, Kathy would ask her how she knew so much, and she would have to confess to listening to her conversations. Kathy would never forgive her for spying.

"No. It's nothing," Haley assured her.

Kathy put her arm around her shoulders. "Well, I'm here if you want to talk."

Yeah, but for how long? Haley thought.

Kathy raised her hand and blew her whistle to get everyone's attention. "Listen up, everyone. There will be a short meeting at the end of practice on Monday. I'll be giving you some information about the upcoming competition, and I have an important announcement to make. Please be sure to be here."

Haley looked at Tori, Danielle, and Nikki. An important announcement. It could mean only one thing. Kathy was going to tell them she was leaving. Soon it would be official, and there would be nothing they could do to change it.

"Hurry up, Haley. Mom's waiting in the car," Tori said as she closed her locker and slung her backpack over her shoulder.

"Go on out," Haley said. "I'll be right there. I'm almost ready."

She was used to riding with Kathy on the afternoons she didn't work at the snack bar, and they were always the last to leave. Today, though, Kathy said she had to get ready for an appointment after practice, and couldn't drive her home. Haley was sure it was with Amy from the Ice Follies.

Haley pulled on her sweatshirt and quickly ran a brush through her thick red hair. Her bangs were starting to look better. She slammed her locker, grabbed her backpack, and hurried after Tori. She was almost at the large glass door to the parking lot when she spotted Patrick walking toward the weight room. She knew Tori's mom was waiting, but she had to talk to him. This was her chance to get him to come to the party. She just hoped he wasn't still mad at her.

"Patrick," she called, running over to him. "Listen, I'm late, but I've got to talk to you. Can I meet you in the snack bar tomorrow night at six-thirty. Please? It's really important."

"Umm. So suddenly I count again," he said. "Well, I think I'm busy."

"But you have to come. Please . . . it's really important," Haley begged.

"Well, maybe I can meet you. But I don't know if I'll be at the rink tomorrow."

Tori poked her head in the door. "Haley. Come on. Mom's waiting."

"Okay. I'll be right there." She looked at Patrick. "So I'll see you tomorrow?"

But he was already walking away without even saying good-bye.

In the car she told Tori how Patrick had reacted. "At this rate, Patrick's not going to show up for his own party," Haley said.

"Why don't you ask Alex or Kyle to help?" Tori suggested.

"Good idea. He's not mad at them," Haley said.

A few hours later, at seven o'clock, Haley, Nikki, Tori, and Danielle stood across the street from Giovanni's. They hoped to see Kathy before she saw them, so they hid behind a truck parked across the street. It was a cold night, and Haley shivered on the dark street.

"Are you sure about what you heard?" Tori asked at ten past seven. Her hands were thrust deep into the pockets of her green parka. "Kathy should be here by now."

"I'm sure," Haley said. "She said seven o'clock at Giovanni's." She heard right, she was sure, but what if Kathy had changed their plans or something, Haley thought. What if Kathy wasn't going to show up?

"Hey, isn't that her car?" Nikki cried. She pointed down the street and Haley saw Kathy's tan Buick turning into the parking lot behind the restaurant.

"That's it," said Haley. "Let's wait another five minutes and then go in."

"And do what?" Nikki asked as they watched Kathy enter the restaurant.

"We can tell her what a great coach she is and that without her we couldn't skate. And maybe Amy will think twice about taking our coach away." Even as Haley spoke she realized her plan was pretty lame. Still, they had to use every chance they had.

"I'm freezing," Danielle whined. "Can't we go inside now?"

"No complaining," Haley said. "Remember, for a good cause you can take a little cold weather." She put her arm around Danielle's shoulders, and the two of them shivered together. "But I have to admit, I wish it didn't have to be the coldest night of the year."

Tori stomped her feet for warmth. "I can't take it anymore," she said. "Let's go in."

The four of them crossed the street and went into Giovanni's.

"All the waiters here know my family. What if they recognize me?" Danielle said. "My parents think we're shopping at the mall. I don't think they'd like it if they found out we walked over here after dark." Giovanni's was a five-minute walk from the mall.

"If anyone recognizes you, just tell them we're looking for Nikki's parents," Haley said. "And pull your scarf up." She adjusted Danielle's scarf so that it covered half her face. "There. Now no one will know it's the famous Danielle Panati."

Inside it was warm, and the smell of spaghetti sauce and garlic bread made Haley's mouth water.

"Oh, wow, I wish we were eating here. It smells great," Nikki said.

Several people waited by a reservation desk for their tables. The girls stood behind the last couple in line. The adults were all dressed up and Haley felt out of place in her jeans, hiking boots, and flannel shirt. Danielle wore a denim skirt, and Tori fit right in with her matching blazer and wool slacks. At least Nikki wore jeans too, but hers didn't look quite so grubby as Haley's did.

The woman ahead of them turned and smiled, "Are you girls meeting your parents?" she asked.

Haley looked at Nikki. "Umm, yes. I think they may be sitting down already."

"Why don't you go ahead of us, then," the woman offered.

"Thanks," said Haley. She grabbed Nikki's arm and pulled her past the reservation desk into the seating area. "Come on. Let's go find them," she whispered as Danielle and Tori followed.

They weaved in and out of the rows of filled tables, looking for Kathy and Amy.

"Excuse me, ladies. May I help you?" said a man in a tuxedo with dark, slicked-back hair. He spoke with an Italian accent, and Haley thought he must be the manager. He didn't sound very happy to see four kids staring at his customers while they ate.

"We're, umm, looking for our parents," Haley said. "They're supposed to be eating dinner here."

"For your parents? You are meeting them here, yes?"

"Yes."

"No."

"Sort of."

They all spoke at once.

"Name?" he asked, moving to the reservation desk.

"I think I see them over there," Nikki said, and the four of them bolted around the manager.

Haley pointed to a table across the room, where Kathy sat with Amy. Haley recognized her from the photo in the newspaper.

"That's her," Haley whispered to the others. "That's Amy."

They hurried across the room to Kathy's table.

"Kathy, hi!" said Haley.

"Well, look who's here." She smiled at the girls as they surrounded her table. "You seem to be everywhere I go."

"We're looking for Nikki's parents. They're eating here tonight," Haley said.

"Were you supposed to join them?"

"No, I just need to get some money. We're doing some shopping over at the mall while they have dinner," Nikki told her.

"Well, I can lend you some money and you can pay me back next week if you want," Kathy offered.

"No. That's okay. I'll find them," Nikki said.

"Girls, I'd like you to meet my friend, Amy Benson," Kathy said. "Amy, these are some of my best skaters." She introduced each of the girls. "Amy is here with the Ice Follies," she went on. "She's the headliner this year. Remember the article I showed you?"

"How long will you be here?" asked Nikki.

"The show runs for nine days, and then we have a break and afterward skate in Philadelphia," Amy said. "I hope you'll be coming to see it."

"Maybe," Tori said with a shrug.

Haley felt like telling Amy to leave their coach alone. Coaching is better than skating in a stupid show, she wanted to say. But she knew Kathy would never forgive her if she was rude to her friend.

"Well, I'll hope you'll come. I'll see if I can arrange free passes for you," Amy said with a smile.

Normally, Haley would have been really excited about free tickets, but now she forced herself to smile and thank Amy.

The girls stood near the table. Haley had the feeling that Kathy and Amy wanted them to leave, but they hadn't done what they had come to do.

"Kathy's a super coach," Haley announced, nudging Nikki to back her up.

Nikki nodded. "The best."

"We couldn't live without her, right, guys?" said Haley.

"Right," Tori added. "We'd die if she ever left."

"No one could take her place," Nikki said. "We couldn't skate without Kathy."

Amy looked at Kathy, and Haley hoped she would say that Kathy should never leave Silver Blades. Instead, Amy said, "All right. How much did you pay them?"

Kathy shrugged. "You guys must want something. What's up?"

"Nothing. We mean it," Haley said. "We just want Amy to know how much you belong at Silver Blades." Then she saw the restaurant manager coming toward them.

"Uh-oh," Danielle said.

"Excuse me, ladies." He bore down on them with a determined look. "You must either take a seat and order, or you will have to leave," he instructed them.

"We're leaving," Tori said quickly.

"What about your parents?" asked Kathy.

"We'll find them," Nikki said.

But Haley couldn't leave, at least not quickly. She moved slowly away from the table, in time to hear Amy say, "Cute kids. They sure are devoted to you. I can see why it's so hard for you to leave."

Kathy sighed. "Even Franz is acting like the place will fall apart without me."

"You're not having second thoughts, are you?" Amy asked her in a concerned voice.

"Don't worry about that," Kathy said. "Everything's all set. Nothing will stop me now."

12

"Thanks for the ride, Mrs. Carsen," Haley said. After Giovanni's they had walked back to the mall, where Tori's mother had picked them up.

Haley ran up the walk and let herself in the side door of her house.

"Haley, is that you?" her mother called. "We're in the den."

Haley went to the den and stood in the doorway. Her mother, Morgan, and Morgan's friend Melissa sat on the couch, their eyes glued to the TV. Her dad was away on a business trip.

It's probably a horse movie, Haley thought.

"What are you watching?" she asked.

"*The Black Stallion Returns,*" Morgan told her.

"Come join us," her mother said.

"No, thanks."

"Oh, by the way," Haley's mother said. "Patrick called. He said something about not being able to make it tomorrow."

"What? He said he can't make it? Why?" Haley asked, her voice filled with panic.

"I think he said something about baby-sitting for his brother." Her mother turned back to the horse movie.

Haley rushed to the phone and dialed Patrick's number, but the answering machine picked up.

Then she dialed Alex's number. "You've got to talk to Patrick," she told him. "The party's tomorrow night!"

"I'll see what I can do," Alex promised.

As she climbed into bed that night, Haley wished she'd never planned this stupid party. Who wanted to have a party when her coach was about to leave and ruin her whole life? And now the guest of honor refused show up. Some party.

"Bad news," Haley told Nikki as the two warmed up at the rink the next day. "Patrick called last night and left a message that he can't meet me here tonight. He has to baby-sit or something. Which means he's not coming to the party."

"What? But he has to come," Nikki said, standing up and stretching her legs. "It's his party."

"I know. Alex said he'll try to talk to him."

"Should we just tell Patrick about the party?" Nikki asked.

"I don't know. Maybe we'll have to."

"Tell who about what?" asked Tori, skating up to the barrier and leaning over it while Nikki and Haley stretched.

They followed Tori out onto the ice and filled her in.

"Well, he's got to come to his own party. I mean, you'll look kind of dumb if he doesn't," Tori said, which made Haley feel even worse. Why did Tori say things like that? she wondered. She knew she didn't mean it, but still.

"There's Alex. Let's find out if he talked to Patrick yet," Nikki said, skating ahead.

Haley started to follow her, when Kathy appeared. " 'Morning. Did you ever find Nikki's parents last night?" the coach asked.

At first Haley had no idea what Kathy meant, but then she remembered the story they had told Kathy and Amy about being in the restaurant. "Umm—we found them as soon as we left. They decided to eat somewhere else instead."

"Amy enjoyed meeting you girls," Kathy said as she poured herself a steaming cup of coffee from her thermos.

Haley nodded. "That was neat." At least, normally it would be, she thought sadly.

"Okay. Let's see. What are we working on today?" Kathy looked at her clipboard. "Only one and a half more weeks until the competition. Let's continue to work on your double axel, and then move on to the footwork in your program."

Haley skated around in a tight circle, trying to visualize the jump. She couldn't concentrate. Her mind kept coming back to the fact that just one day after the competition, Kathy was leaving. Anita Skein would stand where Kathy stood now, telling her what to work on. Haley forced the thought from her head and tried to focus on skating. Finally she went into the jump, putting as much spring into it as she could. As she went up she felt out of balance and knew that she had overrotated her shoulders on the takeoff. She came down too quickly and fell backward.

"Okay. Try it again. Concentrate," said Kathy. "You can do it. You did it beautifully on Monday."

Haley tried again, and this time she managed to complete the jump, but she knew she looked awkward and just barely made it. For the rest of the lesson she tried to think of nothing but skating, but her mind refused to cooperate.

When the lesson was over, Kathy skated up and put her hand on her shoulder. "Hey. Are you okay? Are you sure nothing's on your mind?"

Haley couldn't meet Kathy's eyes. She wanted to tell Kathy everything and beg her not to go. "Well, uh . . ." she began. Then she saw Anita coming toward them.

"It's nothing. I'm just tired, that's all. It was a busy week." She skated off before Kathy could say anything more, and before she could see the tears welling up in her eyes.

As Haley left the ice, Nikki, Tori, and Danielle caught up to her.

"Alex says he's sorry but he couldn't reach Patrick," Nikki said.

"So Patrick's not coming to his surprise party and Kathy is definitely leaving us," Haley said miserably.

"Don't give up," Danielle said. "We'll find a way to get Patrick there, and remember, Kathy doesn't make her announcement until Monday. I think we should tell her we know and ask her to change her mind."

"It's our only chance," Nikki said.

"Okay," Haley agreed as they watched Kathy and Anita leave the ice. "It's now or never."

They quickly left the ice, took off their skates, and followed Kathy to her office. Haley was nervous. She didn't know if this was the right thing to do, but they had nothing to lose. They already knew Kathy was leaving, didn't they?

The girls peeked into Kathy's partially open door. Kathy and Anita stood by the desk. "Kathy? Could we talk to you?" Nikki asked. "Just for a minute?"

"Not right now, guys. I'm having a meeting with Anita."

She started to close the door.

"Wait, we just want you to know how much we need you," Haley blurted out. "You can't go. Really!"

"You guys know about this?" Kathy asked.

The girls nodded. "So it's true?" Tori asked.

"Look. I can't talk now," Kathy said. "But don't worry. It's not such a big deal. Everything will be fine. Now you really have to go."

Kathy shut the door to her office.

For a minute no one said anything. They just stood there staring at the closed door. Finally Danielle said, "So it's definite. She's really leaving."

"No big deal! How can she say it's no big deal? Our coach is leaving and it's no big deal?" Nikki cried.

Haley didn't say anything. She couldn't trust her voice, and besides, what was there to say?

Tori put her arm around Haley. "I'm sorry."

"What should we do now?" Nikki asked.

"When in doubt, eat," said Danielle. "Let's hit the snack bar."

The four of them sat slumped over the counter in the snack bar a few minutes later. Harry saw them. "You girls look like something the cat dragged in," he said. "What's the problem?"

They looked at each other, but no one said anything.

"Hey, cheer up. Whatever it is, it can't be that bad. And anyway, it's Saturday. You kids are throwing the big party here tonight," Harry continued.

"That's part of the problem," Haley told him. "It's supposed to be Patrick's surprise party, only he's not planning to show up."

"What? Not show up? Why not?"

"He's mad at me. He thinks I've been avoiding him

since he hurt his ankle, but I was just trying to organize his party. He was supposed to meet me here tonight at six-thirty, but he said that he has to baby-sit his brother," Haley finished.

"What are we going to do?" asked Nikki. "He has to come to the party. It's for him."

"I think we have to tell him about it," said Danielle. "What else can we do?"

"But that will wreck everything. It's a *surprise* party. How can it be a surprise if he knows about it?" Tori asked.

"Well, it won't be much of a surprise party if the guest of honor doesn't show up," Haley said.

Harry ran his hand across his bald head. "Hmmm. You know, I might be able to help out."

"Really?" said Haley.

Harry nodded. "I can't guarantee it, but I'm pretty sure I know a way to get Patrick here."

"But how?" asked Nikki.

"You just leave it to me," Harry told them. "After all, I am his boss, you know."

"Thanks, Harry," Haley said gratefully.

"No problem, girls. I just want to see some smiles."

Haley hoped Harry's plan would work. The way things seemed lately, she wasn't sure anything would work out right.

13

Haley glanced at the clock on the wall of the snack bar. Almost six o'clock.

"Everyone should be here any minute," she said to Nikki, who finished setting up the table with soft drinks and snacks. Since four o'clock they had decorated and prepared for the party. The room looked great. Streamers hung from the ceiling with balloons tied to chairs. A huge banner printed on Nikki's computer said FOUR MORE DAYS! because Patrick would be able to skate again on Wednesday. The banner stretched all the way across the back of the snack bar. "We're all set. All we need now are the guests."

"Especially the guest of honor," Tori reminded her.

"I just hope Harry's idea works. What if Patrick doesn't show up?" Haley asked.

"Well, we'll just have to party without him," said Danielle.

At six o'clock several kids came in, and by six-ten, the snack bar was packed with skaters, hockey players, and kids from Grandview and Kent. Music blared and everyone talked and laughed.

"I thought this party was for Patrick," Kyle said at about six twenty-five. "Where is he?"

"He should be here any minute," Haley said. "Tori's stationed outside the snack bar, and she'll let us know when he shows up."

"*If* he shows up, that is," Nikki said.

"He better," Haley said.

"I just hope Harry knows what he's doing," Danielle worried.

Just then Tori burst into the snack bar and slammed the door behind her. "He's coming!" she shouted.

"Quiet everyone! Quick! Find places to hide!" Haley shouted.

"Someone turn off the music," Haley called.

"And the lights," yelled Tori.

A few seconds later the snack bar was silent. Everyone waited in the dark listening to Patrick's footsteps come closer. Then the door opened.

"Harry?" Patrick called.

Tori hit the lights and everyone yelled, "Surprise!"

Patrick just stood there staring at them. "What's going on?" he said finally.

"It's a party, stupid," said Alex.

"A party?" Patrick repeated.

"You know, food, music, people, it's called a party," Alex teased.

Everyone started laughing, but Patrick still looked shocked. "But what's it for? I mean, it's not my birthday or anything."

"Doesn't matter," Haley said. "We're celebrating because you'll be able to skate again soon and you won't be such a grouch."

Patrick looked around at the balloons and streamers. "You guys did all this for me?" he asked.

"It was Haley's idea," Nikki said.

Someone turned the music on again, and everyone went back to talking, eating, and dancing.

"You planned all this?" Patrick said to Haley.

Haley nodded. "I know you were angry with me but—"

"I thought you were angry with me," Patrick interrupted. "You kept avoiding me. I thought you didn't want to be my skating partner anymore. I thought . . ."

"You thought I didn't want to skate with you? Why?" Haley asked, so happy that Patrick wasn't mad anymore.

"You were doing so well with your single skating. Landing the double axel and all. Everyone was talking about it." He shrugged. "And who knows how well my ankle will heal? It might take me a while to get back in form."

"Patrick, how could you think that?" Haley asked.

"I don't know. I guess I was crazy. Not being able to skate makes me crazy."

"Hey. We'll always be partners," Haley said.

"We're the best," Patrick said. He stuck out his hand and Haley slapped it, once, twice, and a high five.

She took his hand and pulled him toward the table with the food and drinks. "Come on. Let's get some pizza."

"Great party, Haley," said Jordan, helping himself to his third piece of pizza.

"Thanks," she said, looking around. Everyone was having fun, and it was great to patch things up with Patrick, but she didn't feel like celebrating. After all, her coach's leaving was nothing to celebrate.

Nikki joined Haley and nudged her with her elbow. "Look who's here," she said, nodding toward the door. Kathy and Anita Skein stood in the doorway. Kathy looked around, then walked over to Patrick and gave him a hug. A few minutes later Kathy tapped Haley on the shoulder.

"What a great party. Patrick looks better than he has since he hurt his ankle. He is actually smiling," Kathy said.

Haley nodded.

"You were sweet to think of this," Kathy told her.

Haley didn't say anything. She was afraid if she tried to talk, she might start crying. Kathy eyed her closely. "Hey. This is a party, not a funeral. What's wrong?"

Haley felt her eyes fill with tears. She had to get out

of there before anyone noticed. Instead of answering, she turned and ran out of the snack bar and down the hall to the bathroom.

In the bathroom she splashed some cold water on her face. She hoped no one saw her crying. She tried to pull herself together to go back into the party, but she couldn't face Kathy again. How could Kathy stand there and act like everything was fine? Didn't she care about them at all? Wouldn't she miss them at all?

She took a paper towel and dried her face when, suddenly, the door to the bathroom opened and Kathy came in.

"Okay. What's going on? I may be dumb, but the way you've been acting lately I'd have to be really dumb not to know something was up. Now, tell me," Kathy demanded.

"You're leaving. That's what's wrong."

"You're crying because I'm going away?" Kathy asked.

"It may not seem like a big deal to you, but it is to me," said Haley, the tears starting to come again. "You're the only coach I've ever had."

"But everyone needs a vacation. It's been over a year since I've had one."

"But . . ." Haley started to say, then her mind registered what Kathy had just said. "Wait a minute. A vacation? What do you mean?"

"I'm going on vacation next week, the day after the Regionals. Amy and I are going to Hawaii for two whole weeks. I've always wanted to visit there, and now we finally are. But things here will be fine. Anita's going to take over for me—"

"You mean you're not leaving? You're not joining the Ice Follies?" Haley interrupted.

"Joining the Ice Follies?" Kathy looked at her as if she were crazy. "Where on earth did you get that idea?"

"A vacation? Just a vacation?" Haley grabbed Kathy and hugged her. "This is so great! You're going on a vacation! That's great. That's so great."

"Haley?"

Haley started to laugh. "I don't believe it. All this time we thought you were planning to leave. You were talking about the Ice Follies and about Amy, and then when Anita came, and I heard you say it would be good for us to have a new coach, we thought for sure you were leaving."

"You thought I was leaving for good?" Kathy shook her head. "So *that's* what all the presents and cookies were all about. You were trying to get me to stay?"

Haley nodded. "We thought maybe you felt unappreciated."

Kathy laughed and threw her arms around Haley. "I couldn't leave Silver Blades. Just think how dull my life would be without you and your practical jokes. Why, I'd be bored to tears."

Haley took Kathy's arm and pulled her out the door.

"Come on. We've got to tell the others. Let's get back to the party."

And this time, she thought as she heard the music and laughter coming from the snack bar, I really do feel like celebrating!

#4: Going for the Gold

It's a dream come true! Jill's going to the famous figure-skating center in Colorado. But the training is *much* tougher than Jill ever expected, and Kevin, a really cute skater at the school, has a plan that's sure to get her into *big* trouble. Could this be the end of Jill's skating career?

#5: The Perfect Pair

Nikki Simon and Alex Beekman are the perfect pair on the ice. But off the ice there's big trouble. Suddenly Alex is sending Nikki gifts and asking her out on dates. Nikki wants to be Alex's partner in pairs but not his girlfriend. Will she lose Alex when she tells him? Can Nikki's friends in Silver Blades find a way to save her friendship with Alex *and* her skating career?

#6: Skating Camp

Summer's here and Jill Wong can't wait to join her best friends from Silver Blades at skating camp. It's going to be just like old times. But things have changed since Jill left Silver Blades to train at a famous ice academy. Tori and Danielle are spending all their time with another skater, Haley Arthur, and Nikki has a big secret that she won't share with anyone. Has Jill lost her best friends forever?

#7: The Ice Princess

Tori's favorite skating superstar, Elyse Taylor, is in town, and she's staying with Tori! When Elyse promises to teach Tori her famous spin, Tori's sure they'll become the best of friends. But Elyse isn't the sweet champion everyone thinks she is. And she's going to make big problems for Tori!